ASCENSION OF THE ORC KING

LIONEL HART

CONTENTS

1. Chapter One   1

2. Chapter Two   7

3. Chapter Three   17

4. Chapter Four   29

5. Chapter Five   41

6. Chapter Six   49

7. Chapter Seven   65

8. Chapter Eight   75

9. Chapter Nine   85

10. Chapter Ten   95

11. Chapter Eleven   109

12. Chapter Twelve   119

13. Chapter Thirteen   141

14. Chapter Fourteen   161

15. Chapter Fifteen   177

16. Chapter Sixteen   193

17. Chapter Seventeen   203

Epilogue   217

About the Author   226

Also By Lionel Hart   227

Chapter One

Zorvut

Leaving Aefraya in the cold of the early morning felt entirely different to Zorvut compared to the last time he left the elven capital. Last time, he and Taegan had left together in the warm light of the sunset. Though they had been uncertain and anxious as they had set out that first time, there had been a sense of hope in their resolve that was conspicuously lacking now. Now, he was alone—or, at least, he would be traveling alone. King Ruven was seeing him off, like last time, though his expression was much more dark now in contrast to how it had been then. It had not been so long ago, but it may as well have been in another life for how distant it all seemed.

"They'll only be about an hour behind you, for the most part," the king was saying as Zorvut looked out at the road in the cold morning light, bringing his attention back to the task at hand. "But as you get closer, let them catch up. If you're too far ahead, it won't work."

"Yes, I remember," Zorvut said with a nod, finally turning meet the king's gaze. The elf was standing about five feet away from him, dressed in his usual finery with his hands clasped in front of him. His expression was carefully neutral, as if they were not discussing rescuing his only son, his sole heir. "I've spoken with the captain again, and we've agreed on a series of signals. So we should be able to communicate effectively from a distance even before we arrive at Drol Kuggradh, and I can signal when I'm waiting for them."

"Good," Ruven said, then sighed. His eyes flicked away, for once breaking his emotionless mask and briefly looking as weary and worn as Zorvut felt. "I am entrusting you fully with this, Zorvut. The balance of war and the fate of our kingdom are largely in your hands now."

Zorvut wished he could respond confidently that the king had no need for concern, that he knew exactly how to bring Taegan home safely and end the conflict in one fell swoop. But even if he had truly believed it, he couldn't find the words to say it. Instead, he replied faintly, "Thank you for trusting me."

"Travel safely," Ruven said with a decisive, final nod. He turned and started walking back toward the castle, so Zorvut did not reply, instead turning to face his horse. Graksh't had been standing silently behind him, but he could see the tall stallion's eyes following the king as he left. Though they had been with the elves for many months now and even traveled into human lands, Graksh't still often seemed uncertain of what to make of the smaller figures.

He inspected his saddlebags one last time, though he had packed them himself and checked them once before earlier in the morning. He was traveling light, bringing only his weapons and the barest camping gear he would need for the sixteen days of travel it would take him to arrive at Drol Kuggradh, where the warlord Hrul Bonebreaker was certainly keeping his husband captive. If he were to push himself and his horse, he could probably reach it in half that time, but he had to travel at a pace that the battalion of elves following him could maintain. If he pulled too far ahead, their whole plan would fall apart. Much as it frustrated him to have to slow himself down, it was their greatest hope of success.

Even that left him feeling conflicted. The surest way of ending the conflict was to take out the warlord permanently. But Hrul Bonebreaker had raised him as his son, had been his father up until Kelvhan's betrayal had revealed the truth. The thought of killing, if not his own father, the man he'd considered his father for the vast majority of his life—while his rational mind could recognize it as a necessity, his heart recoiled at even considering it. Even if it were not truly patricide, it felt close enough for him to balk at the thought.

Zorvut shook himself from his thoughts as Graksh't whickered, a low and nervous sound, for he had been standing motionless for several minutes now, staring vacantly out onto the horizon. He could spend the next two weeks mulling it over as he traveled, he told himself, before mounting the horse. Turning back, he took one last look at Castle Aefraya, memorizing its lofty towers of gleaming white stone and the drooping branches of the tree-temple behind it. For all the trepidation he had felt the first time he laid eyes upon the elven city, even then he had thought it was strikingly beautiful. Now, though he hoped it was not, it may very well be the last time he ever looked upon it.

With a commanding shout, he dug his heels into Graksh't's sides, and the horse broke into a gallop past the castle gates and through the main boulevard. A few shouts followed him as he raced out of the city; not cries of anger, but cheers and calls of encouragement. By the king's decision, they had shared no information as to why Zorvut had returned and Taegan had not, aside from the captains and soldiers who would accompany him from a distance, but there had seemed to be some unspoken understanding amongst the layfolk that some plan was being enacted. Every elf he'd spoken to in his brief return to Aefraya—whether the elven generals King Ruven had summoned, or the bartender who served him when he couldn't bear to remain in the castle without Taegan any longer—had all seemed to encourage him, to rally around him, and even now cheered as he galloped out of the city, like some strange symbol of their fighting spirit against the orcs.

Somehow it heartened him and saddened him in equal measure, all at once. If they only knew the truth! He doubted they would cheer for him if they knew how dire a situation their prince was in, how easily Zorvut had allowed him to be taken. He had failed Taegan and, by proxy, had failed all of them. Maybe they would be shouting at him for an entirely different reason, then.

But it didn't matter, he told himself as he approached the northern gate and galloped out beyond its walls. All that mattered now was saving Taegan, bringing him home safely. Everything else was secondary—the war, his own mixed feelings about the warlord—everything.

Instinctively, he felt for the spot in the back of his head where their bond resided. He knew there would be nothing there, just as there had been nothing from the moment Taegan was teleported away, but still he could not stop himself from prodding at it like a tender, painful wound. *Can you hear me?* he thought at it, trying to speak to Taegan the way they would communicate when they were connected. *Are you there?*

There was no answer, not that he truly expected one. As strange and even alien as it had been at first to feel the presence of another in his own mind, now going back to that silence, that emptiness, was unbearable if he dwelled on it for too long. It was not like the raw, bleeding feeling that had throbbed in the back of his head for days when Taegan had severed the bond, what felt like a lifetime ago. In a way, it was a relief that at least he was not in that same agony, but in a different way he almost would have preferred it to the quiet emptiness he had now.

"Stop it," he said aloud to himself, shaking his head. The more he dwelled on it, the closer to the brink of despair it brought him. He took in a deep, steadying breath, focusing on the movement of the strong horse beneath him, the sensation of the cold wind in his hair, only just starting to noticeably grow out from when he had shorn it. Had that really only been a month ago?

He focused on the road ahead of him, running over the map he would follow in his mind. The road would lead him to his husband, and when he found him, he would bring him home.

Chapter Two
Taegan

Taegan was asleep when the faint whisper of Zorvut's voice woke him. *Can you hear me?*

He sat bolt upright, his eyes opening quickly even though he could see nothing in the darkness. *Are you there?*

"I'm here," he whispered before clamping a hand over his mouth, thinking as hard as he could at the spot in the back of his head. *I'm here! I'm here!*

He waited, not even daring to breathe for fear he might miss the response—but no response came. He waited for a minute, and then another. But eventually he slumped down in defeat before laying back in his makeshift bed, a pile of straw with a blanket draped across it. He must have dreamt it. It had sounded so real, but it was not the first time he'd dreamt of his husband in the time he'd been here.

Wherever here was. Though he knew he was in Drol Kuggradh, the capital of the orc-controlled territories and one of the only permanent cities maintained by the roving clans, he could not describe the prison he was in with any certainty aside from the cell that housed him. He was not even sure quite how long he had been here. There was little to do except sleep, so he guessed it had been a few days, perhaps closer to a week. There was no light other than the faint flicker of a torch, maybe two, far down the hallway to Taegan's left, and even that was dim when it was visible at all. More often than not, the torches were not lit, and he was in pitch darkness.

Now that he was awake, hunger prodded at his belly. The orcs had fed him once or maybe twice a day since his arrival, but they were meager meals of water and bread, occasionally cured meats or fruits that were over-ripe and on the verge of rotting. Before Taegan last went to sleep, food had been brought to him by a silent orc whose face he could just make out as being surly and irritated in the flickering light of the torch he had carried, but without knowing how long he'd slept, he might be fed again after another nap or not for several more hours.

He was hungry, and Zorvut's voice in his mind had been so painfully real. Misery settled over him like a heavy weight atop the blanket he'd pulled over himself—and he was cold, too, having been given only an extra blanket against the frigid subterranean mountain weather. The light traveling clothes and sleeping robe he'd been captured in were all he had, and were far too thin to give him any substantial protection from the elements. At night—or at least, when he assumed it was night time—a fire or a brazier was lit far off to the left, where the torches were, where whatever guard watched over them was stationed. That helped a little, but the heat only just barely reached him most nights, taking the edge off the chill but never quite warming him before the faint glow dissipated and died away.

The situation was dire and showed no signs of changing. But what could be done? He had no weapons, no armor, no way of escape—and no chance of fighting off an orc easily triple his weight and nearly two feet taller than him, if not more, even if he could somehow get out of this cell. He had to believe Zorvut was coming for him, a thought he considered both with hope and with dread. Either Zorvut would save him, or they would both die. Hrul Bonebreaker had made that very clear to him in the brief conversation they'd had the night Taegan was captured. All he could do was wait, and hope, and worry.

Taegan had slept so long that now he was restless, unable to keep his eyes closed any longer. He stood and stretched, his muscles aching in protest from disuse, and paced around the cell. It was small for orc standards, but he could get four paces along each wall, making the circuit around the perimeter of the cell over and over. His chest ached with worry and his stomach growled with hunger, but when he focused on his legs moving, the muscles stretching and contracting with every step, he could ignore both unpleasant sensations, and if he counted each step his mind was just occupied enough not to dwell on his bleak present or the uncertain future.

When he had counted one thousand, four hundred and thirty-seven steps, he could hear the loud clanging of the metal door being opened, and he paused, straining to listen. A gruff voice came faintly from far down the hall, speaking orcish. He knew very little of the language but could pick out a few words now: food and water and what he was fairly sure were a few different, formal greetings. Zorvut had tried to teach him a bit of orcish, but always joked his teeth were too small to fit around the words, and he could never get the hang of much more than hello, how are you and my name is Taegan. Neither of those phrases seemed like they would come in useful here.

He thought he heard the word for food from down the hall, then a few footsteps and scraping metal—hopefully that meant he would be fed soon. The voices continued for a bit, sounding like a casual and unhurried conversation. Then, finally, came more footsteps that echoed down the long hallway, and the flickering light was blocked by a hulking shadow.

Taegan took a few steps backward, away from the metal bars where he had been pressing his face a moment before, trying to listen more closely. One of the orc guards often seemed to grow angry at him if he was too close to the door, and he couldn't tell which guard was approaching now, so it was best just to wait at the back of his cell until whoever it was set the food down and locked the door once more.

The guard that approached was not the one that frightened him as much, but still he waited until the orc, never looking over at him, had set down the tray of food in his cell and turned away to the cell in the opposite wall. Taegan stepped toward the tray hungrily, but paused, watching as the orc opened the barred door across from his own and slid a second tray along the stone floor. He had seen food left in the opposite cell each time they fed him so far, but in the dim light that only came from the distant upper room on the left, he could never quite make out the shape of whoever was being held captive alongside him.

The guard said something in a nonchalant tone, but no reply came. He appeared to wait, then spoke again, this time sounding vaguely irritated. A faint voice answered him, speaking only a few words that seemed to placate the guard. Although it had been a long while since he had heard a female orc speak, he thought he recognized a higher, more feminine register to the voice that answered, even though it was just above a whisper.

Taegan frowned as he lifted the heel of bread to his lips, a thought taking him aback. The last time he could recall hearing a female orc's voice had been the illusory figure Kelvhan had summoned when he betrayed them (the first time, he thought bitterly), and that voice sounded vaguely familiar now that he was thinking of it. Had Kelvhan told them that night what had happened to Naydi, Zorvut's mother? He wracked his brain but could not remember—and much to his chagrin, the guard did not try to speak with the other prisoner again, instead locking the door and ambling back through the hallway to the left. His footsteps became fainter and fainter until finally the heavy door creaked closed behind them, plunging Taegan into silence once more.

If Naydi were still alive, and had not been able to flee, it would certainly be plausible that she might be held captive, too. Taegan could easily imagine the warlord not reacting kindly toward his wife upon learning of her infidelity. But it seemed strange he might place them so close to each other—unless it was not intentional, which was a possibility as well.

His hunger won out over his curiosity, though, and he turned his attention back to the food in front of him. Bread, an apple, and for once something warm—a thin soup that was barely more than broth but that he drank greedily before it could grow cold. Even after it was gone, he held the still-warm bowl in his hands for a few minutes, savoring the comforting sensation in his fingers that had been frozen and numb more often than not during his stay here.

The bread was hard, and the apple was mealy, but they sated his hunger for the time being. He pushed the tray between the bars of the cell so it sat just outside, and leaned against the bars to try to make out any sign of the prisoner opposite him. The other captive must have eaten faster than him, though, as he didn't even hear the sounds of eating coming from the opposite chamber, no crunch of an apple or bread. His eyes could not make out any movement, though in the darkness he did not expect being able to see much of anything.

For a long moment, he simply sat there, curled into the corner between one of the stone walls and the metal bars, thinking. If it was not Naydi, would whoever it was get him in trouble for trying to communicate with them? He had already decided his best chance at survival was to put his head down and not make a fuss, at least for now, and the last thing he wanted to do was bring any negative attention to himself. And even if it was Naydi, would it matter? Neither of them could do anything to help the other, he was sure—and he suspected her elvish was likely not nearly at the level of Zorvut's, probably just the same as Taegan's orcish, which was next to nothing.

But he was curious. And maybe they could somehow help each other after all. He wouldn't know unless he tried, would he?

He licked his lips and cleared his throat, unsure of when he had even spoken aloud last. All he could do was try.

"Hello?" he said in a whisper, then paused, waiting, before speaking a little louder. "Hello, is someone there? Can you hear me?"

He waited, sitting perfectly still as he listened intently for a sign of recognition, anything at all from the opposite cell. But nothing came—no movement he could see, no sound of anyone shifting or mumbling or answering in any way. He was speaking in elvish, which probably was not to his benefit, but he wasn't confident enough in his orcish to try to speak it now.

"I'm Taegan," he murmured, trying again. "What's your name?"

Again he waited, holding his breath and listening with all his attention. But again he was met with silence, no discernible sign that he'd been understood or even heard.

With a sigh, he turned away. Maybe he shouldn't have gotten his hopes up after all.

He stood and stretched and resumed walking in an endless loop around his cell. There was nothing else to do.

CHAPTER THREE
ZORVUT

The first few days on the road largely melted together for Zorvut as he traveled, but he did notice when the terrain became more rocky and mountainous, a sign he was approaching the orc territories. Once he was out of Aefraya, he knew he would need to remain more alert.

Traveling at this pace, he had nothing to occupy his time with, so in his mind he went over each of the lessons in magic that his true father, Tomlin Whitmore, had taught him. Though the human was a bard and had not specialized in using his magic as a weapon, there was still plenty Zorvut had learned from him, and plenty more to figure out on his own.

Fire, lightning, ice—Tom had shown him a bit of working with each element, building on his initial, instinctual knowledge of summoning a small flame to his hand and throwing it just a few feet, until finally he could hurl fireballs and light his sword aflame. He could throw lightning bolts like javelins, and with some effort, even bring down a lightning bolt from the sky. Ice was still tricky for him, but he could make snowflakes and throw a handful of sharp glass shards.

But Tom had shown him how to understand his magic in the first place, and he had every intention of working out more on his own. When he thought of the way he summoned fire, he suspected that if he pulled it in the opposite direction of how he twisted it to summon lightning, he might get something like acid, though he was unsure how best to utilize it. He tried it a few times on the road, but conjuring a handful of acid while on horseback ultimately seemed like a bad idea.

The human had been able to explain everything to him in a way that finally made sense, where so many elven magicians from the castle had failed. He was an excellent teacher. It was a shame they had left Tom's home in such a hurry. The thought of that made his chest ache with regret, too—much as Taegan had been restless during their time in Naimere, Zorvut felt quite sure the elf would have far preferred to still be in the port town than wherever he was now. At least, Zorvut thought, he would have certainly preferred it.

The road he traveled started to splinter off into smaller trails and rocky footpaths the farther north he rode—he was familiar enough with the territory that he had no doubt he was still on the main path, but he stopped every so often at a particularly confusing fork in the road to leave a small tower of stones on the side he took. Much as he trusted the elves to find their way, it was best if they were sure of his location, too.

On the fifth day, he was certain he had crossed the border from Aefraya into his homeland. There was no physical marker, no guarded gate or high wall, but something about the craggy shapes that pierced the horizon and the colder bite in the air made him positive he was no longer in Aefraya, with its rolling hills and more moderate climate. Graksh't seemed more familiar with their surroundings, too, though he was sure the only time the horse had ever been this far south on this stretch of road was when they had ridden with the caravan down to Aefraya for his wedding.

The thought of his wedding stabbed his chest with pain. He felt foolish remembering how shy and afraid he had been at first, how much he had dreaded meeting Taegan, and how he would try to avoid his presence as much as possible in those initial weeks. Part of him wished he could go back and relish every second with his husband—the rest of him admonished himself for daydreaming in such a way. Wishful thinking wouldn't buy him any more time with Taegan. He had to keep pressing on.

The sound of horses—not just one, but multiple horses—snapped him from his thoughts, and as he pulled back on the reins to stop and listen, he could tell immediately that the sound was coming from the other end of the steep hill just ahead of him.

Swearing under his breath, he drew his sword and waited. While he was sure he would have to encounter scouts at some point once entering the orc territories, he had not anticipated a fight so soon.

The sound of hooves on the coarse dirt road drew closer and closer, and after a moment he could see the shapes of several orcs on horseback cresting the hill ahead of him. As they drew nearer, he could hear voices, too, jovial conversation and laughter. Whoever this group was, they were not trying to be stealthy. He stood his ground, one hand gripping Graksh't's reins tightly and the other gripping his sword, and waited.

He counted four horses and four figures atop them as they began to descend the hill. It did not take long for one to seem to notice him, and when they did, he could see them stop, the shape of them pointing, leaning closer to their companions—and after a beat of silence, drawing their own weapons. They recognized him.

With a frustrated growl, he dug his heels into Graksh't's sides, and the stallion broke into a gallop, charging the group. He could not risk using his magic, not yet, so he would have to rely on his swordplay. But the group did not look like warriors as they seemed to nervously spread out, weapons drawn but hesitating, waiting for him to approach or for someone else to make the first move. That would work in his favor.

The first strike was almost comical. He did not slow down as he approached, and he could see the startled fear in their eyes as he barreled for the one that had pulled ahead of the other three. The orc lifted a heavy wooden shield in one hand as if waiting to parry Zorvut's strike, but he swung his sword high and caught him right under his chin, opening his throat cleanly. Zorvut circled the group as the first orc fell, his now-riderless horse shrieking and bucking as the body slumped down and slid off, spraying the beast with blood as it sank. Though their animals appeared to be warhorses, none were quite as large as Graksh't, and none as calm at the sight of blood pooling at their hooves. That would work in his favor, too.

Two of the orcs glared at him with hatred in their eyes, both adults, a male and a female. The other was staring at the fallen orc sprawled in the dirt with a fearful expression—a youth, probably no more than twelve—he would leave that one, he decided.

"Cowards," he goaded, locking eyes with the male. The other orc snarled, taking the bait, and kicked his horse into action. Zorvut met him easily, their swords crashing into each other and sliding away as he galloped past before turning around in a tight circle and charging him again. The orc didn't turn his horse as quickly and was only half-facing Zorvut when he pierced him through the ribs, eliciting a howl of pain.

"Bastard," the wounded man spat, clutching helplessly at his wound as he struggled to steer his horse with the hand that still weakly held his sword. The word stung more than Zorvut would have expected, but he only smirked in response, still circling the group at a cantering trot, waiting. The boy was now looking frantically between all three of them, holding a short sword up but with trembling hands.

Now the female roared out a battle-cry and charged, pushing past the wounded male and slashing at him wildly. His shorter stature meant he could easily dodge her attacks as he parried and ducked, and with a hard slash, Zorvut cut the sword from her grip. She screeched, blood pouring from her forearm as the sword clattered to the ground.

"You have no honor!" she wailed as she fumbled with her saddlebag with her one good hand, procuring a dagger that she threw at him. It soared uselessly over his head, and he heard it clatter against a rock on the ground far behind him. "You'll always be a bastard! You'll always be a race-traitor!"

"At least I'll be alive," he snarled, and charged at her again, this time driving his sword forward—it pierced her just under her arm, and her cry of pain was cut short to an empty gurgle as he shoved the embedded sword with all his might and it carved through to her collarbone, not quite clearing to the other side but opening a wide wound all the same. Her horse screamed and galloped away, pulling her off the sword before she fell limp to the ground, dead.

The wounded male shouted as he, too, tried to charge Zorvut, but it was futile. He parried the weak stab easily, driving the blade away from him to circle back with his own and slash him across the belly. The orc groaned and lifted his sword, but he was bleeding out quickly—the strength seemed to drain out of him all at once as the blade slipped from his grasp and he collapsed over his saddle, his consciousness fading.

Zorvut turned to face the boy, who was watching him with his mouth pressed into a hard line over his small tusks but with visible fear in his eyes. He stepped closer to him slowly, holding out his sword covered in blood, but made no move to strike him even as he drew close enough to touch him with the point of the blade.

"What's your name?" he asked. The boy frowned, taking in a few quick, nervous breaths as he seemed to consider the question.

"Vurak," he answered, obviously trying to keep his eyes on Zorvut's gaze and not at the sword pointed at him, but failing.

"Vurak," Zorvut repeated, pulling Graksh't into a slow, measured circle around the boy and his horse. "I don't want to hurt you, Vurak. You don't look like a fighter." The boy flinched at the words. "You're with a group of, what, scouts? None of you were fighters. But you look like you're fast, and quiet. Is that why they brought you along?"

"Yes," the boy croaked, his hoarse voice just above a whisper. "My sister... She brought me. They ordered our clan to scout." He gestured to one of the fallen orcs, the only female.

"Then I have a job for you, Vurak," he continued, keeping his voice low and as nonchalant as he could manage, though the pain and fear in the boy's response sent a pang of guilt shooting through his chest. There was no pleasure in cutting down orcs that were not warriors, as these evidently were not. "I want you to go straight to Drol Kuggradh, and I want you to tell the warlord I'm coming. And I hope you're fast, because if I catch up with you, I probably won't be feeling as merciful as I am right now."

For a long moment, the boy did not answer, just stared at his sword with wide eyes and his chest heaving with rapid breaths. Then, finally, he glanced up to meet Zorvut's gaze, and gave a single, tense nod.

"Good," Zorvut said. "Now go." He prodded the boy's horse with the tip of his sword—not hard, but enough to frighten the beast into bolting. The horse screeched and broke into a run, and the boy struggled with the reins for a few paces before regaining control, pulling it back onto the road and galloping up the hill the way they had come. Zorvut watched him go until he disappeared over the slope; the boy never turned around to look at him.

With a sigh, he dismounted Graksh't and inspected the bodies strewn across the trail. None had weapons worth taking, so he left them for the elves to scavenge. Only one horse had remained, standing nervously at the edge of the road as if waiting for a command, while the other two had dashed away in fear. Zorvut approached the horse slowly and was able to pilfer its saddlebags. But there was nothing of note: a few days' worth of rations and a small amount of coin in a pouch, both of which he pocketed, but nothing else that might be useful to him. So he smacked the horse's haunch and sent it running off into the distance as well with a startled cry.

There would be no point trying to hide the bodies, but he pulled them off the road and laid them neatly along its edge, putting their weapons in a pile next to them. It was unfortunate that they were in the wrong place at the wrong time, but he had a message to send—and most importantly, no one could be left to warn the warlord of the elves following behind him. Much as it pained him, he knew the group of orcs would not have hesitated to cut him down if he had given them the chance.

He thought of Taegan, the terror in his eyes when Kelvhan had grabbed him and magicked him away, and it steeled his resolve. He would kill every orc from here to Drol Kuggradh if that was what it took.

But even as he had the thought, doubt crept into the back of his mind. Scouts and spies he could take on easily, and probably even most soldiers, if he weren't too significantly outnumbered. But he thought of the warlord, and his terrible prowess in battle, the crushing battle axe he wielded... Even with his magic, even as the warlord had slowed in his age, would he be able to kill Hrul Bonebreaker, even if he wanted to? He could not say with any certainty if he wanted to. Maybe there would be another way. Maybe he could convince the warlord to drop his mindless war games, to accept the peace treaty he had been so keen on accepting once before, what felt like forever ago.

The thought did nothing to quell the doubt crawling up his spine, but it was a nice thought.

Behind him, Graksh't snorted and stamped, startling him back to attention. One of the loose horses had started to approach again with some measure of curiosity, but Graksh't's noise spooked it away once more and it galloped off with a nervous whinny.

Sighing, he pulled himself back up onto the saddle and set Graksh't along the trail once more, trotting at a leisurely pace that felt completely out of sync with his own inner turmoil.

It was a nice thought, but a foolish one. Hrul had always been fickle. The warlord would be no more amenable to his words now than when Zorvut had tried to convince him to marry off one of his other siblings instead. Of course, that time it had ultimately worked out in his favor. This time, he suspected, he would not be so lucky.

Chapter Four
Taegan

Though the figure in the cell opposite his own never responded to him, Taegan was becoming increasingly sure that it was, in fact, Zorvut's mother Naydi.

The next time a guard brought food down to them, the guard spoke to the other prisoner again, and the voice that answered sounded very much female to Taegan now that he was listening for it. And the time after that, a different guard was carrying down the food; he must have had poor vision, because he was the one that always carried a torch with him and squinted the whole time. In the flickering torchlight, Taegan got a better look at the orc in the opposite cell, and while he did not immediately recognize her, it did appear fairly close to how he remembered Naydi, at least in the few glimpses he had caught of her in the short time she had been in Aefraya. Surely she must have seen him in the torchlight, too—he was not exactly subtle, pressing his face against the bars of the cell to look as closely as possible now that there was more light in the hallway—but still she said nothing, and that made him uncertain.

It very well could be someone else, he told himself. And even if it was Naydi, it was not so unusual that she might want to distance herself from him, or even be afraid to speak to him. If a guard overheard them, they very well might think they were planning an escape and monitor them more closely, or something far worse. He thought maybe she did not recognize him, but that seemed unlikely—what other elf would be personally captured and held captive by the orcish warlord himself?

But either way, she did not want to speak with him, he told himself, and he shouldn't push his luck. When he was done with the meager meal—bread and a few strips of dried meat again—he curled up on top of his pile of straw, and tried to remember the last book he had read, telling himself the story as closely as he could recall. He was quite sure his retelling was missing some plot points, but it passed the time.

It had been about an hour when sound finally broke through the silence.

"Hello?" a faint voice came from the opposite cell in heavily accented elvish, and Taegan jumped in surprise—if his bed were not already on the floor, he certainly would have fallen out of it. "Hello?"

"Hello," he hissed, barely able to keep his voice at a whisper as he clambered up from his pile of straw to press his face between the bars. "Can you hear me?"

"Yes," the voice came back, hesitant this time. "Don't speak much elvish. You speak orc?"

Taegan bit his lip in frustration. "No," he replied in orcish, wracking his brain for any stray bits of the language Zorvut had shown him or that he might have heard in passing. "Um, hello, my name is Taegan."

An amused snort answered him. "No orc then," the voice came quietly, speaking elvish again. "Just elvish. I know you. My name is Naydi."

"I knew it!" he hissed, resisting the urge to smack the metal bars in front of him in vindication. "I knew it was you. Why didn't you answer me before?"

"Dangerous," she replied, and in the darkness Taegan could barely make out the shape of her shifting to sit against the bars of her cell as well. "They hear elvish, they..." She made a noise from the back of her throat like a bone being snapped. He could understand that without words, at least.

"Okay," he said, nodding in agreement. "Okay. That's alright. I can be quiet. Gods, you have no idea how badly I've wanted to have someone to talk to."

"Listen," Naydi interrupted before he could start babbling. "Listen. I know why you here. Hrul took you... Because me. I did bad thing. My fault." She paused, but even in the silence Taegan could tell there was more she wanted to say and could not put into words he would understand. "I'm sorry, you, Zorvut. My fault."

Taegan pursed his lips before letting out a long sigh. That alone seemed like reason enough for her to hesitate to speak to him. And, in truth, part of him did bristle at the thought of her place in all this—though she couldn't possibly have known then how her actions would snowball. Mostly, though, he yearned to have someone to talk to, to commiserate with, to just prove to himself he was not so maddeningly alone in the darkness. It was not his place to forgive her, but as far as he was concerned, her actions were far more pardonable than what Hrul had done to them.

"Well, thank you," he replied slowly. "I think Zorvut would value hearing that more than me, but... For what it's worth, I appreciate it."

"I'm sorry," she repeated softly. They sat in silence for a long moment; now that he finally knew it was Naydi, Taegan was unsure of what else to say to her.

"Zorvut will come," he said quietly. "He'll come for both of us."

"No," Naydi answered sharply, and Taegan looked up in surprise, though he could not quite see her. "No, if he comes here, Hrul kill him. He can't."

Taegan frowned. Zorvut was certainly on his way, and he, at least, was sure that he would win whatever fight lay ahead. But she seemed far less sure, though she had no idea about the magical ability he'd spent the last month honing.

"He'll be alright," Taegan replied. "He'll win."

Naydi said something in orcish that he could not understand, but the worry in her tone came through clearly. She obviously did not believe him.

"It'll be alright," he insisted, and she fell silent. "He'll fight, and he'll win."

She made a faint grunt of acknowledgment, but did not respond. He could not think of anything else to say, and so they lapsed into silence for a long moment.

He was ready to crawl back to his makeshift bed, their conversation seemingly over, when her voice finally came again from the darkness.

"You have elf magic?" she asked, her broken elvish tinged with hope. Taegan winced at the question.

"No, I don't," he replied quickly, looking away although it was too dark to see her at all. "I don't know any magic. I'm sorry." If he could do even basic magic, that could change things, but he was certain even the warlord knew he had no magical ability to speak of—if he hadn't known, or even only suspected Taegan of hiding some latent magic, his hands surely would have been bound to his sides from the beginning.

"No magic," she repeated slowly, and sighed. The disappointment in her voice was palpable even from

Taegan's cell. For a moment, he wanted to blurt out that though he did not, Zorvut did—but he thought better of it. If he were Zorvut, he would be relying on the element of surprise that his newfound power would bring, so the fewer that knew of it, the better. Could he trust her with that information? He wanted to, but he wasn't certain, so he held his tongue.

Taegan waited to see if she would say more, but now she seemed truly done, a heavy silence settling over them.

Dejectedly, he settled down into his pile of straw, pulling the blanket over him. Though the two blankets were thin, luckily they were orc-sized, so he could place one over the straw and then fold it up to cover his legs and torso while wrapped up tightly in the second. If he laid on his side and curled his legs up a bit, he could pull the second blanket all the way up to his chin. A small comfort, but a comfort nonetheless.

He mulled over their conversation for a while, absorbing everything Naydi had said. It was the first conversation he'd had in what felt like years. He thought he would have been more eager for a long discussion, but there was a hopelessness to the orc woman's tone that had permeated her words and left him unsettled.

But he couldn't let that cause his own hope to waver, he told himself. He knew what Zorvut was capable of, far better than she could have known. Zorvut was coming for him, and would fight for him, and would win.

The thought of Zorvut caused his mind to move instinctively to the silent bond in the back of his head. When his thoughts were occupied, he could ignore it well enough, but most of the time it had a strange sting to it, a prickly emptiness that he couldn't put into words.

He had not heard Zorvut's voice again since the day it had woken him from his sleep, as clearly as if the half-orc had spoken in his ear. He had tried thinking at the spot where the bond sat with all his focus and concentration, trying desperately to convey a message or hear even a whisper of Zorvut's thoughts, but it was a fruitless endeavor. It must have just been a dream after all, but the thought certainly didn't stop him from constantly thinking back to his words and fixating on the empty point in his head. What else was there to do?

I'm here, he thought, focusing on it once more. He mouthed the words silently as he thought them, squeezing his eyes shut in concentration. *Please, if you can hear me, say something. I'm here.*

But, of course, there was no reply. He knew that was not how the bond worked, that the magic that connected them simply had a limit to how far it could extend, and that wouldn't change, no matter how hard he concentrated on the words. As real as Zorvut's voice had sounded then, it was a dream. It sounded real because he was afraid, and missed him, and yearned to truly hear his voice. But it was a dream.

Taegan sighed and gave himself up to sleep.

Taegan did not hear Naydi speak again until the next morning, or at least after he had slept, if that could be called the morning. He had been awake for a little while and was pacing in circles around his room when her soft voice broke through the sound of his footsteps.

"Taegan," she murmured from the opposite cell, and he stopped. "Taegan."

"I hear you," he answered in a low whisper, shuffling over to the bars. He still could not quite see the woman, just the faint outline of her.

"You want out of here?" she asked, and Taegan blinked in surprise.

"I mean, of course," he replied after a beat of hesitation. "I don't see how, though. Do you have a plan?"

She grunted in reply, seeming to mull over her words before explaining. "Wait too long, Hrul come kill me, us. Better die trying to get out instead of die here." She paused, Taegan remaining silent as he processed her words. "If you come, I try get us out. Jump on guard. He only has one dagger."

"What?" he finally blurted, his mind racing. She wanted to try to escape? Even if they could subdue a guard, then what? How would they get out? How would they leave the city? He wasn't sure what to ask first. "You're really going to try to escape?"

He could hear her scoff, or maybe she was laughing at his shock. "I try. Yes."

"Even if you do get the jump on the guard, how are you going to sneak out? Where would you go?"

"Take clothes, sneak out," she replied, sounding far more nonchalant about it than he would have, all things considered. "Go north. Or if you come, go south to elves. Maybe."

"Maybe," he echoed weakly, glancing nervously to his left, where he knew the guards were stationed. There was a door separating them, but now he worried it was not enough to mask their conversation even though they spoke in elvish. "And how would I sneak out? Something tells me there aren't many other elves here."

"Hmm," she replied slowly. "I wrap you up, carry you. A package."

He laughed aloud at that, clamping a hand over his mouth. The absurdity of it all was starting to sink in. The thought of trying to leave sounded insane, but was it any more so than just sitting here and waiting for whatever fate had in store for him?

"Okay. Okay. Let's say we could get out of town," he said, lowering his voice as much as he could physically manage. "Aren't there patrols on the roads? We would have to make sure not to be seen at any point."

"Yes," she agreed. "Danger, yes. Risk. But possible."

"And where would you go? What's up north?" he asked.

"Wilderness," came the reply. "Camp out until fighting is over. Or new plan."

Her nonchalant tone, even in their quiet whispers, was somehow maddening to him, but he felt almost manic in the way he had latched on to the idea. If they could escape, if it was actually feasible, then shouldn't they put every effort into doing so? And even if he were apprehensive of the idea, if she did somehow escape, would he truly be able to just sit back and watch her go?

"No, no," he said, shaking his head, although he knew she could not see him doing so. "Just hiding out isn't a good plan. And you'd have no supplies, no camping gear... You'd still die." Naydi snorted again and started to protest, but he bowled over her. "But if I were with you... If it were me, I would go into Aefraya, but not south. All the orc forces are going to be heading south toward the capital. They'd catch us for sure. But there's an elven outpost to the east, right on the border, outside the Forest of Solitude. It's not big enough to be a threat. No orcs would be marching on it, not now. And it must still be manned by at least a few elves. I'd go there."

"You'd go there," she echoed, the unspoken question hanging in the air between them for a long moment. She could not go there alone, and he would never be able to break out of the prison without her.

"And you really think you could take the guard? And the one up the stairs, too, or however many there are?" Taegan asked, his voice lowering conspiratorially.

"I was warlord's wife. I fight anyone," she boasted, then after a moment added in a more uncertain tone, "If I surprise him, yes. If timing bad... maybe no."

That wasn't exactly much to bank on. But, uncomfortable as it was to admit, if she failed to subdue the guard, he could feign ignorance of her plan and likely be unaffected by it. At least, that was what he hoped, but it was more a guess than anything.

"Okay," he breathed, still uncertain. "Okay. You really want to do this?"

"Better than dying a prisoner," she replied. Even in the pitch darkness, she did not hesitate; her resolve came through clearly without Taegan needing to see her face. She was going to try no matter what, it seemed, so he might as well try to help. Her succeeding alone sounded unlikely, but maybe together they would have a decent chance of living to see beyond their prison once again.

"Let's do it, then," he murmured, and he could practically hear her grin from across the hallway. Nervously, he glanced toward the left where the stairs were again, though nothing had changed since the last time he'd looked toward them. "When? Today?"

"I try today, but just if... good time," she answered, clearly struggling for words. "If good, yes. If bad, wait."

"Should I try to distract him? While he's opening your cell, maybe? I could try and yell or something, so he turns away from you."

"No, no," she said. "I don't think so. I think just wait. Too loud, scare other guard. One at a time."

"Just wait," Taegan repeated, and sighed. "Alright, then. Gods, I hope this works."

Chapter Five
Zorvut

The path through the orcish territories toward Drol Kuggradh was the loneliest Zorvut could ever remember traveling. Though he had purposely chosen a route that meandered through the rocky foothills to avoid as many villages and camping grounds as possible, the lack of any sign of civilization still somehow took him by surprise. He hardly even saw any travelers on the road—but that was just as well, as the two groups he encountered after the first had met the same fate.

They all recognized him easily, but none could match him in battle. With the second group, he spared one more, giving her the same command to alert the warlord of his arrival before sending her off. With the third, all three were soldiers, so he lit his sword aflame to fight, and that meant all three had to die. The less Hrul Bonebreaker knew of his newfound ability, the better chance he had of surviving their inevitable encounter, he told himself, though part of him still held some small hope that mercy might win out in the end.

Other than those three groups of scouts and soldiers, he did not see another soul in his travels. Once, he saw what he initially thought might be a lone hunter on horseback in the distance, but it turned out to simply be an exceptionally large elk. Normally he would not mind the solitude, but now it felt maddening.

He had been on the road for just over a week and estimated he'd more than passed the halfway point when he heard the sound of hooves approaching again—but when he stopped to listen, they were coming from behind him, not ahead. The sound was too light, too rapid to be one of the larger warhorses the orcs rode. His heart sank as he turned to look behind, and sure enough, a helmeted elf was riding up the trail toward him atop a slender, speckled gray horse. That couldn't be a good sign.

Zorvut stopped and waited for the elf to approach. When the figure pulled off his helmet, Zorvut recognized him—a captain by the name of Kyrenic, who had been the first to arrive when King Ruven had initially summoned the closest captains and generals to him. They had a friendly rapport and Zorvut liked him well enough, but if he was seeing him now, then something must have gone wrong. The elf's mouth was pressed in a hard, grim line as he approached.

"Zorvut," the elf called, pulling back on his reins so his horse slowed to a trot next to him. "I bring news."

"Kyrenic," Zorvut replied as politely as he could manage. "Tell me."

"The orcs have moved on Castle Aefraya, truly this time," the elf said with a sigh, looking out to the horizon ahead to avoid meeting Zorvut's gaze. "They estimate close to a thousand, and several villages have already been evacuated. The King has called back half the forces marching with us, to help prevent a siege by striking from behind."

Zorvut scowled, looking away as well. Though it was not entirely surprising, his chest burned with frustrated disappointment anyway. Losing half the battalion was a blow; an unexpected show of force might have made the warlord think twice about continuing to put up a fight, if nothing else, but with only half the amount of warriors he'd been relying on, a change of plans was inevitable.

"I see," he replied slowly, unable to find any other words.

"I don't know if our original plan will hold up as well with a smaller force," the elf continued after a beat of silence. "So I've come to ask if you want to proceed as planned, or try to adjust somehow."

Zorvut appreciated his candor, if nothing else. There was no way to mince words about it—half their forces pulled away meant their plan depended that much more on him and him alone. If he failed, his safety net was now only a fraction of what it would have been.

But what else could he do? He had come this far. Turning back now, leaving Taegan behind—he may as well fall upon his own sword then and there. Every nerve in his body ached to be reunited with his husband, his bonded mate, the other half of his soul. He couldn't turn back now, even if he wanted to.

"Thank you for alerting me," he said slowly, meeting the elf's gaze. Despite Kyrenic's stern demeanor and grim expression, he recognized a look of concern in his eyes. "This will make our job more difficult, but I can't turn back now. I'm going to continue as planned. If anything, this will allow for us to travel a bit faster." He paused, considering. "Tell whoever's left that if they value protecting their home more than following me, they have my blessing. I'll make do with whoever remains, but if the castle is truly in danger, I can't ask them to come with me."

The elf tilted his head as he looked up at Zorvut, as if surprised by his answer, but his expression did not change. He seemed to mull over his words for a moment before finally answering. "I'll pass the message along. I promise you my sword, if nothing else, though I'm sure more than a few will still want to do what they can for the prince. I know my warriors were... eager for such a prestigious mission. You won't go alone."

"Thank you," Zorvut replied faintly, nodding once. "Have you already sent back the half the king asked for?"

"Not yet, but General Daphine and I were going to decide how to split the group tonight and send them off come morning. We've just received the missive no more than an hour ago now. The general sent me on ahead to tell you shortly after the courier arrived. I'll have to ask how she will want to proceed once I get back," Kyrenic said, glancing back down the road as he spoke.

"Don't let me keep you, then," Zorvut said, gesturing. The elf hesitated as if he wanted to say more, but stopped himself, then nodded.

"I'll come find you if anything else changes, but it's best if we still keep our distance," he said, and Zorvut nodded in agreement. "Otherwise, we'll see you at Drol Kuggradh."

"Yes," he agreed, but Kyrenic was already pulling his helmet back on and nudging his horse, trotting down the way he came before breaking into a gallop. Zorvut watched him leave until he could no longer make out the shape of the elf atop the horse in the distance, then finally turned away and set forth once more with a long sigh.

Beneath him, Graksh't grumbled, sensing the sudden downturn in his mood. He patted the horse's neck absentmindedly, but he was more than occupied with his own thoughts. While it was not the worst news he could have received, it was certainly not good news, either. He wondered if Hrul had always planned to move on the capital, or if it was a direct response to his forewarned arrival. Not that it mattered at this point—it would be a thorn in his side, regardless. All he could do was trust King Ruven and the other elves to hold fast until he made it to Drol Kuggradh and, hopefully, put an end to everything.

Much of the plan had relied on him before, but now it rested that much more entirely on his shoulders. If he could not subdue the warlord, he could no longer fall back on the force of elves to take the city by surprise.

Zorvut bit his lip—he had realized it when Kyrenic first spoke, but it was sinking in more fully now. They had taken the decision away from him, along with his hope. He no longer had any choice in the matter. With their weakened forces, if the clash turned to army against army, they had little chance against all of Drol Kuggradh's forces, even if Hrul hadn't gathered more warriors to him as Zorvut suspected he had.

But single combat for the title of warlord would very well be an even match. Hrul was still bigger and stronger, but though he was no elder, he was also no longer young, a far cry from the frightful warrior who had killed the leaders of so many other clans and bound them to his own.

If he could keep the upper hand fighting one-on-one, with the extra surprise factor of his magic... If their plan had any chance of success, he would have to be the one to kill Hrul Bonebreaker.

CHAPTER SIX
TAEGAN

Taegan spent little time sleeping after his and Naydi's conversation, too nervous to do anything other than pace around—though there wasn't much else to do, anyway. His mind was racing, playing out as many possibilities of their plan as he could imagine. If they managed to subdue the first guard, and the second up the stairs, and if no extra guards were standing watch, and if they could be decently disguised so that no one recognized them, and if Naydi could get them past the city gates without anyone stopping them, then they would probably be alright. But whatever lay beyond the walls of the city, he couldn't account for. They had been underground so long, and he'd been magicked to Drol Kuggradh so suddenly. He couldn't say with any certainty what the weather would be like, but he assumed probably cold in the mountains, especially if they would go northeast toward the elves. That could be a problem. All he had aside from his blankets was the loose sleeping robe and pants he'd been teleported in, and his boots he had slipped on in a hurry. It was cold even down here, and if he wasn't walking around his cell, he was wrapped as tightly as he could manage in the rough blankets atop his pile of hay to keep warm. Even if they could steal the guards' clothes, if it snowed...

But it would only be a few days to the elven outpost, he thought, even by foot. It was right along the edge of the northeastern border between the orc wildlands and the very northernmost point of Aefraya. Drol Kuggradh was quite far to the north as well, but he was fairly sure that there was no path leading directly to the outpost, so it would be difficult to judge when they would need to veer off the main road and out into the wilderness. That could cost a few extra days. And again, if it snowed, it would significantly slow them at best, and kill them at worst. If the gods had any mercy for him at all, it would not snow.

He thought about Naydi's plan to carry him out of the city. That seemed the only option as far as he could tell, as he certainly could not walk out. He would bet all the gold he had back in Aefraya that he was the only elf in Drol Kuggradh, so there would be no mistaking who he was for anyone who might see him. They had nothing except what they could find here, but he would have to stay hidden somehow. He could curl up enough that she could probably wrap him up in the blanket, or maybe a bigger piece of fabric or clothing if there was one somewhere on the upper level. It would just depend on what they could scavenge, and if Naydi could take on the guards. Maybe if he could get his hands on an orcish shortbow, he would be able to help, but that was unlikely.

All in all, it seemed like the odds were stacked against them. The guard could kill Naydi, or they could be recognized in the city, or a band of wandering orcs could find them on the road or in the wilderness, or they could succumb to the elements. Was it worth the risk?

Taegan desperately did not want to die there. He did not want to die at all, of course—he wanted to go home to his husband, his family. But if he was going to die, Naydi was right—better to die fighting than dying a helpless prisoner. He was sure Zorvut was coming for him, but he could not say with any certainty how long he had been here, or how long it might take Zorvut to arrive. Maybe, if they were able to escape and made good time, he could prevent Zorvut from needing to make the dangerous journey at all.

That was the hope he would cling to. They would escape, and he could spare Zorvut from having to come to such a dangerous place, from having to come confront the warlord in his home. Whatever came after that, they would deal with then. If he could get back to

Zorvut and help ensure his safety, then the risk would be worth it.

But now all he could do was wait. So much of the plan was out of his hands, so he kept pacing and thinking and trying to account for as many scenarios as he could imagine.

It had been several hours when he finally heard the unlatching of the door up the stairs to the left. For the first time that he could remember since being imprisoned here, he felt warm, almost sweaty, though it was surely just because of his nerves. He shot a nervous glance toward Naydi's cell, but in the dim darkness he could not see her at all.

The door swung open, and a bit of flickering torchlight reached them—it must have been the orc with the poor eyesight who always carried a torch. Usually he gave Taegan his food first, which was perfect. If things went badly and Naydi wasn't able to subdue the guard quick enough, he figured he could throw the tray through the bars as a distraction.

Sure enough, the guard turned toward him first as he descended the stairs, balancing two trays on one arm as he held the torch in the other. Taegan watched from the back corner as the orc set down one tray, fumbled with the ring of keys attached to his belt, unlocked his cell, swung open the door, pushed the tray of food inside, and closed the door once more to lock it again.

He grabbed the food off the tray—bread and cheese this time—but kept his eyes trained on the guard, his heart pounding.

Taegan glanced over at Naydi's cell again as the guard turned away. This time he could see her in the torchlight, standing at the bars of the cell. She met his eyes briefly before glancing up at the guard, who paused at her door. Although his back was turned to him, Taegan could imagine him scowling at Naydi as he barked something in orcish and she took a begrudging step away. This seemed to satisfy him, though, as he shuffled the keyring and the second tray between his hands, unlocking her cell.

The guard bent down to set her tray on the floor, and that was when she lunged at him, leaping to tackle him to the ground while he was off balance. There was a shout and a clatter as they tumbled onto the plate of food, and Taegan dashed up to the bars of his cell to watch more closely. The guard's torch fell to the floor, too, casting the two struggling figures in a dim flickering light as the flame sputtered.

He could just make out the orc's mouth, open and trying to shout, but Naydi had worked quickly to get him in a chokehold, pressing her full weight onto the guard's neck. Desperately, he reached up and grabbed Naydi by her hair, and she howled in pain as he yanked, struggling to rip her off of him.

Taegan dropped the bread he was holding, picked up the metal tray, and wedged his arm between bars. It was difficult to aim, but he flung the tray as hard as he could manage. Despite his archer's eye, though, the tray hit the guard in the knee—it made a painful metallic clanging sound at the impact, and a choked noise of pain escaped from his gritted teeth, but it didn't seem to dissuade him from digging his fingernails into Naydi's scalp.

Even from this distance and in the dying light of the torch, Taegan could see blood streaming down her forehead from where he was clawing at her. But she made no sound beyond that first initial, startled cry, her arm still wrapped firmly around the guard's neck, and after what felt like an eternity his movements slowed and stilled, and finally she released him, letting the orc's limp body collapse to the ground.

Taegan didn't realize how hard he was breathing until they fell into silence when the guard's movement stopped. The torch had almost gone out, but there was just enough light that Taegan could see Naydi wipe blood from her eyes as she straightened over the unmoving form.

"Not good," she muttered, and in the faint light he could see her eyes glancing over at him. "Not good. Let's move fast."

"Toss me the keys," Taegan said, his voice still a low whisper. She bent down to pull the key ring from the guard's body—whether he was unconscious or dead, Taegan couldn't tell—and tossed it in the direction of Taegan's cell. The keys clattered along the dirt floor, sliding up to the metal bars, and he winced at the loud sound before reaching through to grab them.

The angle was tricky, and he wasn't sure which key exactly was the right one, so it took some trial and error before his cell door finally unlatched and he pushed it open with a euphoric rush of adrenaline. Though he knew he wasn't free yet by any stretch of the imagination, he certainly felt freer just opening the door. When he looked back over to Naydi, she had stripped the guard of his uniform and pocketed his dagger, and was shoving the hunk of bread that had fallen to the floor into her mouth. That was smart—he glanced down at his own food and took a bite of his own bread. After all, he had no idea where their next meal might come from.

"Stay quiet," Naydi murmured, stepping through the door of her cell. "Still one more."

And as if on cue, from the left side of the long hall, he could hear the wooden door unlatching and swinging open, and he swore under his breath as they both looked down the hallway, then back at each other. An orcish voice called out, and he froze in a panic. What now? Could they fight off another orc, without the surprise that had given Naydi the advantage with the first one?

"Give me keys," Naydi hissed, and the urgency in her voice made him toss the keys back to her without a second thought, even as his brows furrowed in confusion. In the flickering torchlight, her expression looked positively grim. "Listen. You not know about my plan. I force you out. Understand?"

He nodded, but it took a beat for him to process what she was saying—before he could reply, though, the voice called out again, and now he could hear footsteps coming from the stairs. Taegan slunk backward into the cell, and Naydi gave him one last inscrutable look before turning back to the door and charging, bellowing something in orcish that he did not understand. But the sounds that followed were understandable even without language; a startled shout, a scuffle, what sounded like more footsteps coming from above, and then light flooded the hallway, making Taegan wince. A multitude of voices were shouting now, but the light was blinding to his eyes that had grown so accustomed to the darkness. He stumbled forward to peek through the open door, unable to bear not knowing, but could barely make out the blurry shapes of several more orcs. Most were carrying torches, trying to haul Naydi off another guard who she had pinned to the ground.

His heart sank all the way to the bottom of his stomach at the sight, taking any hope of escape down with it. With that many guards together, even if she could somehow fight them all off, their escape certainly would not go unnoticed. As his vision adjusted to the new light, he could make out one of the orcs, this one without a torch in its hands, raising a weapon—something blunt and heavy, maybe a mace—and bring it down hard over Naydi, and he couldn't tear his eyes away as the sickening, recognizable crack of bone breaking pierced the air, followed by a shriek of pain. Even from this distance, he could tell her arm was broken with the impact, sticking at an unnatural angle as they finally wrenched her off the guard she had grappled. With his clearing vision, he could see four orcs, plus the one on the ground now stumbling to his feet. If there had been that many in whatever building the dungeon was attached to, then they had never really had any hope of escaping at all.

Two of the new orcs with torches were hauling Naydi to her feet, dragging her up the stairs, but the first guard pointed down the hallway with one hand as he dusted off his clothes with the other—pointing toward him, Taegan realized with a start. The orc with the mace started walking toward the cells, and fear seized him as he stumbled all the way to the back of his cell, pressing his body up against the cold stone wall. The hulking figure appeared in the doorway, and the orc scowled as she pushed open the unlocked cell door. She shouted something in orcish, the other guards shouted something back, and the orc stepped inside the cell.

"I didn't do anything," Taegan stammered anxiously, his eyes on the orc's mace. "Please, I didn't—"

The orc snapped something in reply, but he didn't understand any of the words, so when she reached down to grab him by the wrist he didn't resist, letting himself be pulled out of the cell and stumbling to keep up with the guard's much longer stride. One orc stayed behind, checking the guard Naydi had attacked, but from the quick glance he spared, Taegan still could not quite tell if the orc was alive or not.

The two orcs carrying Naydi were already gone by the time the guard had dragged him down the length of the hallway, and as he was hauled up the steps, she unceremoniously lifted him off his feet and slung him over her shoulder. Much as he wanted to protest against the indignity, Taegan kept his mouth shut—but it worked out just as well, as the sun was blinding when the guard carried him outside. Blinking and wincing against the glaring light that burned his eyes, which had long since adapted to the pitch darkness of the dungeon, he could now only feel the movement of the orc walking with no idea where they were headed.

Eventually, his vision adjusted enough that he could make out the shapes of their surroundings, but without warning, he was tossed to the ground, the wind knocked out of him as he landed on a hard stone floor. The world spun dizzyingly around him for an unbearable moment, only the cold stone beneath his face keeping him grounded. He could hear soft whimpers of pain near him, then a louder gruff voice speaking in orcish—when he could focus his eyes, he could see Naydi huddled on the ground and curled around her broken arm maybe ten feet from him, and fear struck him anew at the sight of the warlord crouched over her and hissing something through gritted teeth.

Hrul swung his massive shaved head to look in Taegan's direction, scowling openly down at him as he pushed himself up into a sitting position.

"Little elf," he growled, stepping toward him, and this time there was no mockingly playful tone to his voice but only a cold, barely restrained anger. "What were you planning?"

"Nothing," Taegan panted, barely able to catch his breath. "I don't know—she just attacked the guard and unlocked my cell. I don't know what she planned."

Hrul's eyes narrowed; they were nearly the same golden-yellow shade of Zorvut's eyes and for an instant, Taegan bristled with hate to look at them. They weren't even related—he had no business having the same color eyes as Zorvut.

"I don't believe you," Hrul replied slowly, deliberately, as he stepped around Taegan in a narrow circle. "You knew it was her? You spoke to her?"

"I—I suspected," he stammered, following the warlord's slow circuit with his eyes. Naydi had not been that far ahead, but he was unsure how much information he might have gotten from her in that time. He had already gambled with one lie, but he could still dance around the truth. "And then—yes, I knew it was her. But she doesn't know much elvish, and I don't speak any orcish. We barely spoke. Just enough to... to know who we were."

"Yet you did not know anything about her plan to escape. How... convenient," Hrul said with a scowl. "I thought you were smart, little elf. I had hoped you would avoid becoming a thorn in my side, but here you are." He leaned further over Taegan as his voice dropped lower and more dangerous, and much as he wanted to shrink back, to run away, he forced his muscles to stay still, meeting his furious gaze. The warlord remained in the same intimidating pose for a long moment, clearly searching Taegan's face for any sort of tell, but everything within him was screaming to not give him anything.

Finally, the orc straightened, a sneer still on his face as he spoke. "Even so, you're of more use to me alive than dead. You're lucky I won't kill you for now, but remember your days are numbered." Without warning, he reared his head back and spat in Taegan's face.

Taegan bit back a curse, flinching as he turned away, and he forced himself to take in a long breath before lifting his hand to wipe his face clean with his sleeve. Hate and humiliation burned through his veins in equal measure, but when he opened his eyes again, he could see Hrul had stepped away from him and was addressing the guards who had brought them, gesturing angrily between Taegan and Naydi. The guards shrunk back, looking cowed—he guessed his suspicions that the warlord was not aware of how closely they were imprisoned were correct.

Finally, Hrul turned away from the guards, back to Naydi, before rearing back and kicking her in the ribs. Taegan winced, and Naydi wailed in pain, shrinking away from the warlord with a sob. He growled something, low and dangerous, and Taegan did not need to understand him to know it was a threat. Wordlessly she nodded, and he snapped his fingers toward the guards, two of which came hurrying over to haul her away again.

Now that his eyes had adjusted, Taegan could see they were in some sort of stone building, narrow and rounded—maybe a tower? The bare floor beneath him was cold, but he could hear a fireplace crackling somewhere nearby, and as he followed the warlord with his eyes as the orc walked away, he could see into an adjoining room where several more orcs were sitting around a wooden table, looking toward the scene with idle curiosity.

Hrul wasn't looking at him—the remaining guards were focused on his tirade—and the orcs in the other room were distant. The door behind him was closed, but not locked.

He would never get another chance like this again.The thought seized him, and adrenaline pulsed through him—he knew he had no possibility of making it on his own, but for a wild instant he started to scrabble to his feet, trying to get to the door without the orcs spotting him.But he hadn't even fully stood up before the same guard had lunged over, grabbed him by the arm, and hauled him away, making him stifle a yelp of pain as the sudden force felt like it might dislocate his shoulder. The orc barked something harsh, and Hrul answered with an equally irritated-sounding utterance before sneering at Taegan.

"Stupid little bitch," he muttered in elvish, stepping forward to grab Taegan's face with one hand, pulling his chin up to force their eyes to meet. "You think you'd survive a second out there?" Taegan glared at him, willing every bit of hate he could muster into his eyes.

"He's going to kill you," he snarled, struggling against the orc holding him. Hrul's grip tightened, sharp nails digging into his cheeks, enough that Taegan could feel blood welling on his skin. But when he winced, the warlord laughed and turned away with a dismissive wave of his hand before speaking in orcish once more.

Again the orc manhandled Taegan over her shoulder and carried him out of the building, and as they left Taegan looked up to see that they had indeed been in a stone tower, maybe three or four stories tall from what he could tell. The guard carried him through the wide streets of Drol Kuggradh, and despite his furious tears blurring his vision, he tried to look around at his surroundings. He could see more orcs staring at him with wide eyes and uncertain expressions—though they were clearly unarmed, visibly citizens of the city, somehow meeting their eyes was deeply uncomfortable. After a moment, he kept his gaze trained on the ground instead until the light disappeared around them and he was brought back underground.

Again he was thrown unceremoniously back into the cell, and in the flickering torchlight the guard carried, he could see that all evidence of the struggle in the opposite cell was gone. He suspected Naydi would not return, not now that Hrul knew they'd been so close.

Once the guard had locked the cell and gone back up the stone steps, he was once again in darkness, this time truly alone. His heart still pounded with adrenaline, making his limbs tremble as he huddled into his pile of straw and wrapped the thin blanket around him. Somehow his brief moment in the light, cruel as it was, made the dark feel even more oppressive now.

Chapter Seven
Taegan

He did not see Naydi again. While he had seemed to get off lightly at first, Taegan soon realized he was being punished, too, though through much less violent means. He had no accurate gauge of time, but it felt like well over a day before he saw another guard, and when the orc approached, he carried only a torch and a pitcher of water.

"W-Wait!" he stammered as the orc moved to leave after setting the water on the ground in his cell, and the guard glanced back at him but did not stop. He could hear the harsh footsteps getting further away, going up the stone stairs, and finally the heavy wooden door swinging closed once more. With shaking hands, he lifted the pitcher of water to his lips and took a small sip, but despair had filled him anew and he feared he might be sick with anxiety despite the hunger gnawing at his belly.

Usually, he would walk around his cell for a bit, but this time he crawled back under his blanket atop the pile of hay. If he were asleep, he thought, he wouldn't feel like he was starving, and the time would pass faster. Hopefully.

Sleep didn't come easily, but eventually, the darkness took him. Still, it was a fitful, restless sleep, though at the very least he did not dream of being hungry. He woke once with his stomach still aching, but he kept his eyes closed and remained motionless under the blanket, and at some point it faded away again with his consciousness.

He dreamt of being home, with Zorvut, but always the comfort of his dream melted away to fear, visions of the castle being overrun and blood bathing its walls, and in his dreams he was searching desperately for Zorvut, for his fathers, for anyone—yet found no one. But he did not dream of being hungry.

It was the metallic clatter of his cell door opening that snapped Taegan awake a second time—he sat bolt upright with fear, though the adrenaline faded into relief as he caught sight of an orc holding a torch setting a tray of food down a few feet away from him, glancing over at him with an irritated disinterest. The moment the door had closed again, he scrambled over to the tray. It had only two slices of buttered bread and a cup of water, and some part of him bristled with frustration at the meager amount of food, but the rest of him was too hungry to care, scarfing it down as quickly as he possibly could.

When the food was gone, his stomach still yearned for more, but the sensation began to fade as he slowly sipped the water until he'd drank it all, then crawled back to his makeshift bed. He was still hungry, but it took the edge off enough that it felt easier to fall back asleep. What else was there to do now?

Just before he could sleep again, though, another noise roused him; from the hallway came the sound of the heavy wooden door opening. Taegan frowned as his eyes opened once more. Why had the guard returned, and so soon? It couldn't have been more than an hour, even with his entirely uncalibrated sense of time.

But as the footsteps approached, even in the darkness he could tell that the orc was not the same as the guard that had just been there—he did not carry a torch—and he sat up uncertainly as the sound drew closer. Sure enough, an orc he didn't recognize appeared in front of his cell, unlocking the cell door without explanation.

"Come," he said gruffly once it slid open, adding something in orcish that he did not understand. Taegan waited, uncertain, then the orc spoke again, sounding far more irritated this time. "Now!"

That did not seem promising, but Taegan acquiesced, stumbling to his feet to step toward the guard. The orc grabbed him by the shoulder and pulled him from the cell, before pushing him toward the stone steps where another guard was waiting, this one the same orc with the torch who had just brought him food. He could see the torchlight glinting off a set of metal chains in his opposite hand, and his stomach lurched with fear.

The first orc held his shoulder with a painfully strong grip as he stepped up to the second one, who yanked his right wrist up, wrapping the chain around it. Taegan offered his left hand, but still the guard grabbed him as roughly as if he were trying to flee. His wrists were wrapped so tight that he winced as the guard locked the chain in place, but did his best not to make a sound. He would not give them the satisfaction of knowing he was afraid or in pain, though his heart was pounding in his chest.

Once he was sufficiently bound, the first guard took the length of chain and led him up beyond the stairs, through a small room that Taegan barely got a glimpse of before pushing open a heavy metal door and flooding Taegan's vision with light. In the time since he had last been brought out of the dungeon, his eyes had readjusted enough to the darkness that now the sunlight made his head throb and his eyes burn. He winced and stumbled after the orc, who was walking on completely unfazed.

Taegan followed blindly for a long moment, blinking and rubbing his eyes as much as he could with his wrists wrapped so closely. Tears streamed down his face as if he were weeping, making what little he could see blurry and shapeless for a long time as they walked. When his vision finally adjusted, they were still outside, yet none of his surroundings were familiar.

But as he glanced around, the streets seemed vacant—had it been so empty before? He could not quite remember. He knew that Drol Kuggradh, though it was the largest city in the orc territories, housed only a small population of permanent orcish residents, as the majority of their number still roved the mountainous wilds as nomads. They might pass through the capital on occasion, but rarely stayed for long. Still, something about the silent, empty roads unsettled him.

Taegan managed a glance up at the sky—luckily, the lack of high towers and tall buildings meant he could see the sun unimpeded, although the brightness of it burned his eyes anew. It was a clear day, and the sun was quite high in the vivid blue sky, just a bit off from the center. Whether it was late morning or early afternoon, he could not tell.

He had to jog to keep up with the orc as they walked, making a few turns but mainly following a wide dirt road in a straight line. It looked like they were approaching the city gate.

Taegan's heart leapt into his throat at the realization. The city gate? Certainly they would not be releasing him, but where else might they take him? But as they drew nearer, he could distantly hear voices speaking the harsh, guttural sounds of orcish words. Something must be happening.

Sure enough, as they approached, Taegan could see a clearing in front of the city gate, and a crowd of orcs had gathered around it. He recognized the warlord Hrul Bonebreaker standing in the center, speaking to some of them. Unlike the last time he had seen the warlord, he seemed ready for battle now, his face and body covered with red symbols in stark contrast to his dull green skin and a massive battle axe strapped to his back. Now that he was looking, many of the orcs that were crowded around him looked dressed and painted for combat as well.

Taegan's heart sank down to the very pit of his stomach. If the warlord was preparing for battle, then...

"Ah, the prince has arrived!" Hrul Bonebreaker exclaimed in elvish, his eyes landing on the approaching guard that lead Taegan toward the clearing. Much of the chatter around them fell silent at his voice, heads swinging to stare at Taegan as well. He barked something in orcish, making a beckoning gesture at the guard, before continuing in elvish, "Excellent. Come here, come here."

The guard leading him lowered his head as he approached, then handed the chain over to the warlord before stepping away silently. Taegan eyed him warily, trying to keep his face void of any emotion despite his pounding heart.

"I'm sure you must have questions," the warlord continued, grinning down at Taegan. "And I'll indulge you, since we're waiting for our entertainment to arrive."

"Please, enlighten me," Taegan replied wryly, looking away. The orc chuckled, turning to face the city gate and gesturing toward it.

"Everything has worked out exactly as I'd hoped," he went on. "Poor, guileless Zorvut has made his way here all alone and should be arriving within the hour. Soon, he'll arrive, and when he does, you'll watch me kill him, and then you will die, too. Then nothing will impede my siege into Aefraya."

Taegan forced his face to remain still, forced his breathing to remain slow and calm. But his heart was pounding, his stomach roiling with nerves. Part of him was relieved Zorvut had come to rescue him, but the rest of him was terrified. The warlord was so much bigger, so much stronger—did Zorvut really stand a chance, even with his magic?

"Or maybe I'll make him watch first," Hrul said, glancing back down at Taegan with a sneer, clearly irritated at the lack of response. "What do you think? Should I behead you right away, or should I make him watch you be fucked to death? I'm sure more than a few of these men wouldn't turn down the opportunity to try."

Fear spiked in chest at that, and he could not stop the words as he snapped, "Why are you doing this? Why are you trying to punish him for something that isn't his fault?"

"It's only partly about him," he answered, the casualness in his voice sparking even more rage in Taegan. "He was supposed to be my excuse to end the peace treaty, anyway. I had hoped you would find each other insufferable and eventually he would return. But then he had the gall to side with you damned elves, so you all have to go."

"It sounds to me like you're trying to punish him for your wife's own indiscretions," Taegan replied bitterly.

He did not see the warlord lash out at him, but suddenly he was on the ground, the wind knocked out of him and his face throbbing. His nose was bleeding, he realized as he pressed his bound hands up to his face and pulled them away wet and bloody. When his eyes trained on the warlord hulking over him, Hrul's face had finally twisted into a look of true rage.

"She will continue to pay for what she did, too," he snarled, then wrenched on the chain, hauling Taegan to his feet. Blood splattered down his neck and onto his shirt. "But I have more important matters to deal with first."

Part of Taegan wanted to make some retort, but the words died in his mouth. Something clicked in the back of his head, and there was a sense of unease that was not his own coming from the bond.

Zorvut. Relief flooded him so rapidly that tears immediately sprang to his eyes, and he pressed his hands to his mouth. With any luck, Hrul had not seen the grin that had instinctually spread across his face. He doubled over, his whole body shaking as he tried to stop himself from weeping in sheer happiness. It was as if he had been viewing the world through a cloudy lens that had finally been pulled away and, for the first time in weeks, he could truly see.

Zorvut must have felt the bond snap back into place, as well, because the anxiety that had been trickling from the bond suddenly became a joyful relief that echoed his own.

I'm coming, he heard in his head, as clearly as if Zorvut were whispering in his ear. *Trust me.*

"Finally sinking in, eh?" Hrul said, now with a faint grin spreading around his tusks. "Unfortunately for you, no one here will be moved by your tears."

Taegan barely heard him, his entire consciousness cradled around the pinpoint in the back of his head where Zorvut had finally returned, where he belonged. A spark of hope bloomed in his chest, for once overpowering the fear that had been simmering inside him from the moment he had been captured. Zorvut would save him, he knew it. He had to.

Chapter Eight
Zorvut

The morning he knew he would arrive at Drol Kuggradh, Zorvut dreamt of Taegan.

His thoughts had often been on Taegan, of course, as he had had little else to think about in the two weeks he had been on the road, even more so since his conversation with Kyrenic. With such a grim purpose and no traveling companions other than his horse, what else could he have focused on? But he had not dreamt of his husband in the way he did that morning, still so early the sun had not yet risen.

It had felt so real, as if they were really back home in their room, their bed. As he woke, he felt almost ashamed for having such a dream on a day like this—he had fallen asleep the night before thinking this could be the last time he settled down to sleep, that he very well might die before the next sunset, and *this* was on the forefront of his mind?

Though, he thought as he laid sleepily under the stars with his eyes half open and his erection straining against his loose sleeping clothes, if he was going to perish today, there was something to be said for being able to enjoy almost fucking his husband one last time. Gods, it had felt so *real*, so familiar, down to the curves and angles of Taegan's body, how impossibly tight and wet he was around him, the expressions on his face and the sounds that spilled from his lips. It was a shame he had woken too soon.

But it *was* a dream, Zorvut chastised himself with a sense of finality, and he squeezed his eyes shut and breathed in long, slow, even breaths until his cock lost interest and he started to doze off again. Already, though, his nerves were buzzing with anxious energy, and while he rested, he did not fully fall back to sleep. Soon, the rising sun on his eyelids told him it was time to get up and break camp.

The thought of food made him want to vomit, but he forced down a few mouthfuls of hard bread and water. He could not remember the last time he'd really felt hungry at all, but he would need more than just adrenaline if he had any hope of surviving to see the sun set that night.

The surrounding light of the dawn was still soft and new when he broke camp and set Graksh't on the trail. His surroundings were looking more and more familiar as he approached the parts of the orc territories where he had spent most of his life. It would be a few hours yet, but today was the day.

As he traveled, he tried to keep Taegan's face in his mind's eye, trying to replicate the elf's smug grin when they sparred, the soft look of tenderness he had in his eyes when he read aloud for Zorvut in their private study, the way his eyebrows knit together when he was at the height of pleasure. That one was easier to remember. But despite his efforts, he constantly found himself thinking back to the last time he had seen Taegan in the flesh, his wide eyes full of fear as he had reached fruitlessly for Zorvut to protect him. It pained him nearly as much as it kept him moving. He wouldn't fail again.

When Zorvut could first see the faint shape of Drol Kuggradh in the distance, its spiky guard towers spread out along the city gates rising above the sparse trees and rock formations on the horizon, he dismounted to cover himself and his horse with war paint before continuing any further. The symbols of battle adorned his shoulders in red, spreading down his chest, and he smeared his face with vertical lines coming from his eyes. His hair was still too short to tie back, too long on the sides to paint his head, but he would have to make do with what he had. On Graksh't, he painted symbols of luck and fortune, wards against harm, and the meaning of his name—a champion, a victor.

He knew he would face the warlord in just a few brief hours, and either he would kill the man who had raised him to win back his husband, or he would die. A sense of dread filled him when he thought of either option.

Zorvut took a deep breath to try to center himself before climbing back atop his horse and continuing slowly toward gates of Drol Kuggradh. He would need to be close enough that the elves behind him could see the city, but not so close that the orcs standing guard would spot them and reveal his hand. So he moved slowly, watching the shape of the gates in the distance cautiously for the moment he could first discern any signs of life atop them. From this distance, he could only just make out the vague form of the towers rising above the skyline, but the trees were sparse and thin, without providing much cover. He could not draw too close.

He was still nearly a mile away from the gate when something snapped in the back of his head, a jolt of pain and fear—not his own, but Taegan's.

"Taegan," he gasped aloud, pulling back on the reins to stop Graksh't from moving any further. He clamped a hand over his mouth and squeezed his eyes shut against the tears that suddenly stung against his eyelids, but the relief he felt at the reconnected bond was overwhelming. His husband was alive. He was injured, he was afraid, but he was alive, and close enough that he could feel his presence.

Taegan must have felt it, too, because the fear that had first trickled into his mind was quickly replaced with a crashing wave of relief that mirrored his own.

With every bit of focus he could muster, Zorvut directed his thoughts toward the bond. *I'm coming. Trust me.*

Taegan's response was much more abstract, but a general sense of acknowledgment and acceptance came from their bond, still with the backdrop of overwhelming joy and relief. Despite himself, Zorvut laughed aloud. All at once, every moment of suffering he had endured up until this point was more than worth it. How had he survived this long without the bond? It was as if he had been holding his breath for three weeks and now, finally, could fill his lungs with precious, life-giving air. For something he had not known existed up until the minute their bond was formed, he could not imagine ever living without it again.

"Okay," he whispered to himself, trying to clear his head without much success. "Focus."

Still light-headed, he nudged Graksh't's sides and set the horse trotting forward again. He had a little further yet to go, a little longer to wait. He had to stay focused and sharp. A jagged seed of fear still gnawed at his belly, but for now it was far overshadowed with his relief, his love. For Taegan, he could do anything.

Finally he could start making out movement along the wall, patrols of orcs moving back and forth. He stopped where he was and waited. Though he could not see the elves behind him, he knew that they would spot him long before he had any inkling of where they were, and would send him the signal once they were ready.

Part of it still did not feel real. Taegan was here, he could sense him once again through the bond, and he was about to parley with the warlord. What could he say to the orc that might convince him to change his mind, to pull his forces away from Aefraya and return to the terms of the peace treaty they had once agreed upon? Even with his newfound hope, he was not sure there was anything he could say to Hrul Bonebreaker that might change his mind. He had come prepared for war, and that was what he would most likely get.

He had been standing and waiting, watching, for close to half an hour when he finally got the signal—three calls of the Aefrayan bluejay, with its distinctive lilting chirp that was never heard north of the border. The birdsong steeled his resolve, and with the knowledge that whatever elves remained would now be waiting on his signal, he kicked Graksh't into a gallop toward the city gates.

They were open, though he was sure it was a taunt more than it was a welcome. He was spotted quickly, glancing up at the gates again to see orcs watching him, pointing and gesturing, but none made a hostile move toward him. They were expecting him, just as he'd hoped, and he heard from the nearest guard tower the bellowing horn that must have been alerting the warlord of his arrival.

Zorvut breathed as slowly and evenly as he could manage atop his galloping horse, keeping his eyes trained on the trail ahead of him. It would do him no good to watch the guards watching him now.

He slowed to a quick trot as he approached the open gate, and slowed even more as he saw a crowd gathered just beyond it, all dressed for battle and looking toward him. The crowd of orcs had assembled in a semicircle within view of the gate, and in its center stood the man who had once been his father, the warlord.

Hrul was painted for war just as he was, his head shaved and painted with every symbol of war and battle and conquest that Zorvut could recognize and some he could not quite make out at this distance. His massive battle axe was strapped to his back, and a smug smirk was on his face as Zorvut approached, pulling back on the reins to hold Graksh't in place.

Zorvut's eyes locked on Taegan and despair filled him for a brief moment—the elven prince seemed so small next to Hrul's hulking presence. His delicate hands were chained together and leashed to the warlord. His clothes were dirty and torn, and what looked to be fresh blood covered the lower half of his face and the upper half of his shirt. Even from this distance, he looked gaunt and haggard. But his husband's eyes were wide and gleaming as they saw each other, and Taegan smiled at him.

He managed a slight smile, too, before looking back toward the warlord and pressing his lips into a hard line.

"I've arrived," he said simply, calling out with as commanding a voice as he could muster. The surrounding crowd was completely silent.

"I welcome you, Zorvut," the warlord answered in a mocking tone, opening his arms. "We've been expecting you. I appreciate your forethought by announcing your presence. If you had arrived unannounced, we wouldn't have been able to set up this welcoming party for you."

"I thought you might appreciate it," Zorvut replied wryly, narrowing his eyes. "I have no desire to play games with you, Warlord, and you are still the man who raised me. So I'll ask you this once. Return my husband to me, and recommit yourself to the peace treaty you signed, and we can all move past this as allies."

There was a beat of silence, then Hrul's head tipped backward and he laughed aloud, a howling, disdainful laugh that told Zorvut with absolute certainty how futile his words were. He should not have been surprised, but still it felt like a small part of him—the hope that the man cared for him at all—died at the sound.

"We both know that isn't going to happen," he finally answered, shaking his head incredulously when his laughter had faded away. "No, you're both much more valuable to me dead than alive."

Zorvut closed his eyes and took in a long, slow breath.

"Then you leave me no choice," he said, and slowly he dismounted from Graksh't. He could hear some of the orcs in the crowd surrounding them ready their weapons as he moved, but the warlord seemed unconcerned with a smug smile still on his face, and no one made a move toward him. "I challenge you, Hrul Bonebreaker, to single combat according to the ancient ways. I challenge you for your title of warlord."

"Ha!" the orc spat, his delighted grin somehow spreading even wider around his massive tusks. "I have to hand it to you, I was hoping you'd say that. A bold choice! Zorvut the Relentless, I accept your challenge."

CHAPTER NINE
TAEGAN

Taegan's heart pounded in his chest anew at the words—though he still heard them in orcish, Zorvut's understanding of them through the bond was enough for him to know what had been offered. When Zorvut had asked to end things without bloodshed, for one wild moment, he had hoped against hope that he might convince the warlord, that the orc might be moved by his words, that his heart might be made soft seeing the child he had raised.

But he should have known better. Hrul Bonebreaker had proved himself time and again to be a cruel man out for blood. As he spoke in acceptance of Zorvut's challenge, he threw the chain binding Taegan to the ground—he took a few nervous steps backwards, the length of the chain trailing as he moved, but an orc standing behind him stepped forward to pick it up, meeting his eyes with a warning glare.

From the bond, he could feel Zorvut's weary acceptance, mounting fear, and unbroken resolve all at once. As grim as his countenance was, there was a strange confidence in his stance that allowed Taegan a glimmer of hope. Zorvut briefly met Taegan's gaze and gave him a curt nod of acknowledgment, then drew his greatsword, moving into a ready stance. He had told Taegan through the bond to trust him—he had to believe he knew what he was doing, that he had a plan.

A tense silence fell over the crowd as the orc and half-orc stood opposite each other, both with weapons drawn and circling the other, waiting for whoever would make the first move.

Finally, Hrul spat at Zorvut's feet. "Enough of this," he snarled, and he lunged at the smaller half-orc, swinging his battle axe down on him with a roar.

Zorvut dodged him deftly, leaping away so the battle axe landed uselessly on the ground and bounced back up with the force of the swing. Without missing a beat, he leapt forward to meet him again, swinging his greatsword as the warlord lifted his axe just in time to parry the strike, the sound of steel on steel breaking through the tense quiet.

What was he waiting for? Why was he not using his magic? Taegan frowned as he watched, unable to pull his eyes away from his husband as the two figures pulled apart and circled each other again, weapons raised. He did not understand, but he had to trust Zorvut had a plan.

Part of him wanted to call out to him, to beg for him to end this, but he didn't dare open his mouth. Every orc around him looked just as focused and just as silent—whatever this one-on-one combat symbolized, it seemed they had no intention of interfering, at least not yet.

"Come on," Zorvut goaded, and with a roar, Hrul lunged at him once more. Zorvut raised his sword to parry but the force behind the axe knocked the blade back uselessly, and he was barely able to dodge the cruel strike. The edge of the axe brushed against his upper arm, opening a thin wound. Zorvut winced, but otherwise seemed unfazed. He took a few steps back and finally glanced down at his sword. Taegan recognized the look of concentration, and grinned as the weapon burst into flame, eliciting several startled gasps from the surrounding orcs.

Hrul was silent, but hesitated for a brief moment, his eyes flicking between the burning blade and Zorvut's face with furrowed brows. But Zorvut gave him no time to consider the revelation, lunging toward him again, swinging the sword up. Hrul met it with his axe, but the flames sent a shower of sparks and embers spraying into his face. He turned away with a shout, shaking his head, and Zorvut swung at him again, this time catching him in the shoulder. There was an audible sizzle as the sword burned his flesh and he stumbled back.

"A party trick," Hrul snarled, stepping away to glance at his wound before looking back over at Zorvut. His face had transformed into a hideous glare, his nose wrinkled with tension and his lips pulled taut around his tusks. "Meaningless now."

"Of course," Zorvut answered wryly, but he lunged at him again; this time, Hrul dodged rather than parried. But Zorvut was smaller, faster, and he swung again and again in rapid succession until Hrul could not jump back quickly enough, the sword piercing his side. He grabbed the sword where it pierced him instinctually, his face twisting in pain as he pulled Zorvut closer, raising his axe in one hand and swinging it down with a crash.

Pain exploded through the bond as the blow threw Zorvut to the ground, though he kept his grip on his sword that remained alight. Taegan winced but clamped down the cry of pain in his throat before it could escape. Hrul looked down at his hand, visibly burnt and glistening red, before glaring down at Zorvut at his feet with the wind knocked out of him.

"Get up," he growled, and kicked Zorvut in the ribs. Taegan felt it as sharply as if he were the one being kicked and could not stop a gasp of pain from escaping him, but Zorvut stumbled to his feet anyway, wiping blood from his mouth as he stood. He swung the sword back up into a ready stance, still burning with flame, and silently met Hrul's gaze. Even from this distance Taegan could see Hrul all but glowering in rage, seeming to finally take Zorvut's challenge seriously. Something about his demeanor, his stance, had changed entirely.

With a roar, Hrul leapt at him, hammering him with blows that seemed impossibly fast for how large the battle axe was. Zorvut parried more than a few, showering the warlord with embers with each strike, but many still struck him, slicing open his arms and torso with shallow, bleeding wounds. After a flurry of attacks, the warlord kicked him again, shoving him backward—Zorvut stumbled, but did not fall. Taegan could see his chest heaving as he panted for breath, the red of his war paint becoming indistinguishable from the blood that coursed over his body, and for a moment the hope he had felt was snuffed out like a candle.

His own body tingled with the remnants of pain that made it through the bond. More than ever, Taegan was suddenly sure he was going to watch his husband die in front of him, and he bit his lip to keep himself from crying aloud.

From a distance, he could see Zorvut's eyes flick toward him for only an instant before looking back at Hrul. It was fainter this time, but again he felt from the bond—*trust me*. Taegan swallowed his tears and nodded, keeping his eyes trained on Zorvut.

"Yield," the warlord growled. His voice was low, dangerous, but in the heavy silence around them it projected as much as if he had shouted the command.

"Never," Zorvut spat, and leapt toward him with a violent slash. The warlord dodged, stepping back—and instead of lunging for him again, Zorvut jumped away as well, creating distance between them. Hrul hesitated, uncertain, and as Taegan watched, Zorvut glanced up at the sky for a brief moment, his brows furrowing in concentration.

But before anything could happen, the warlord roared something in orcish that Taegan did not understand, and terror erupted from the bond as Zorvut shouted in reply, swiveling his head toward Taegan.

Taegan froze, uncertain, but before he could react, the orc holding the chain that bound him yanked back forcefully and he stumbled backward into the taller figure. With a gasp that was quickly cut off, the orc's powerful arm came around to pin him into a chokehold, lifting him off the ground by his neck. Instinctively, he kicked as hard as he could, writhing against the guard and digging his fingers into the flesh of his bicep until they drew blood, but the orc seemed to barely even flinch.

The pressure around his throat was so strong he thought his neck might snap before he suffocated. Even as he kicked uselessly, all he could feel was the tight pressure building in his lungs and his face, his mouth open and straining to bring in any air at all, mouthing silent words to cry out and beg for help, for mercy—was this really how he was going to die?

His vision was quickly going dark. Distantly he sensed fear and rage pouring through the bond, but it felt muted and faraway, slipping away from his focus.

And then—there was a roar of flame and a searing heat, and all at once the pressure around his throat was gone as he fell to his knees. He gasped and coughed as cold air flooded his lungs, his vision snapping back into place as heat burned up his arm; he would have cried out in pain if he weren't rasping for breath, one hand coming up to smother the flames that licked up his sleeve and seared his skin. It wasn't enough—something snapped in the back of his head and he threw himself back onto the ground, smothering the flames between his body and the dirt. When the flames were gone and panic had stopped ringing in his ears, he could hear shouting, scuffling.

When he looked up again, a steady stream of fire was pouring from Zorvut's hand onto the orc who had been choking him, who screamed and fruitlessly tried to stumble away—and from behind Zorvut, Hrul charged up and brought his axe down into Zorvut's back, sending him to the ground with a pained shout.

Agony burst through the bond, and he bit back a sob as it only made his burnt arm sting all the worse. "Get up," he exclaimed, though it only came out as a hoarse whisper. "Get up!"

And as if he had somehow heard, Zorvut flipped onto his back and shot a stream of fire in Hrul's direction. It missed, but gave him enough time to stumble back to his feet. A crazed look of fury was on Zorvut's face as he rose, unlike anything Taegan had ever seen from him before, and he spat something in orcish full of vitriol. Hrul scowled and answered, but Zorvut's eyes had already left him, looking back up into the sky again. Zorvut lifted his free hand a, and with his eyebrows knit together with effort, made a pulling motion as his hand closed into a fist.

From the clear, cloudless blue sky, a bolt of lightning came screaming down, so bright that for an instant the city seemed dark as twilight in comparison. The deafening bolt crashed directly above Hrul Bonebreaker, drowning out his shout of agony as it struck him cleanly between the shoulders. He collapsed to his knees from the sheer force of it, his face twisted in pain, and as Zorvut stepped closer to him, he could not move, his muscles quivering and tensing uselessly. He was stunned, immobile, and for a drawn-out moment,

Zorvut only stared down at him. Taegan could feel a swell of emotions through the bond—regret, and sadness, and fear, and through it all the rage that was plain on his face, and more quietly beneath that, an unyielding resolve that had never wavered.

Zorvut lifted his flaming sword above the kneeling warlord, and with a roar of exertion, brought it down full force. There was no sound as he severed the warlord's head from his body, rolling to Zorvut's feet before the spasming mass collapsed to the ground in a pool of gushing blood.

Chapter Ten

Zorvut

He had done it. The air around Zorvut felt eerily still and silent as he looked down at his father's body—no, not his father, but the warlord. The eyes were still open on the severed head and almost seemed to twitch and spasm as if looking around in terror. It must have been a trick of the light. The orc was absolutely dead.

Zorvut finally wrenched his gaze away from the corpse to look over at Taegan, who was staring back at him from where he had fallen in the dirt with wide eyes, mouth agape. He could not quite sense what he was feeling from the bond; the whole world seemed to be holding its breath, as if waiting for him to act before shifting back into motion.

The elves. The signal! The thought snapped him from his stunned reverie, and he tore his gaze away from Taegan to look up once more, forcing all his focus into wrenching another bolt of lightning from the sky. He could feel the flames surrounding his sword sputter and die as he channeled all his magic into a bolt of heat, twisting it into lightning and pulling it down from the atmosphere in a thunderous crash, then with a herculean effort, pulled down a third. His muscles quivered and ached, and when the earsplitting bolt had rumbled and died away, he allowed himself a brief instant to slump forward and breathe in, expanding his lungs as much as he could.

There was still more to be done. He had to finish the plan.

From where he was leaning down, he reached out and grabbed Hrul's severed head by the ear, hoisting it above his head as he stood up straight in spite of his aching muscles and stinging wounds.

"The warlord is dead!" he shouted in orcish, projecting his voice as far and as loud as it would go without breaking. "I've bested him in single combat! Throw down your weapons or die!"

The silence surrounding them finally broke with a few nervous murmurs. Several were glancing nervously between Zorvut and the burnt body of the orc who had been holding Taegan's chains, dead on the ground. Among the crowd, there was the clatter of a few swords dropping. Even as some dropped their weapons, though, others scowled and glared, looking between Zorvut and those who had yielded. He could feel their eyes on his wounds, his chest heaving for breath.

"You can't strike all of us down with a thunderbolt, traitor," one orc in the crowd spat as he stepped forward, axe in hand.

Zorvut smirked. He had hoped someone would ask.

"Those weren't for you," he replied, and pointed back toward the city gate. "It was for them."

A confused hush fell over the gathering of orcs, and in the quiet he could hear it—the thundering beats of many horses galloping right for the city gates. Zorvut did not look behind him but watched the faces of the surrounding crowd morph into shock and even fear with an unrivaled sense of satisfaction. Against all the odds, he had pulled it off. He'd done it.

Though it would have been that much more fearsome if the full battalion he had been planning on having with him had arrived, nearly two hundred elves all on horseback were still nothing to scoff at within the city walls. Their weapons were drawn, but they stood at the ready as they gathered around, and he recognized Kyrenic's dappled gray horse pulling up next to him, the helmeted figure looking toward him with a sword in one hand.

"I tell you again," Zorvut called out in orcish. "Drop your weapons! Your warlord commands it!" He glanced over at Kyrenic alongside him and said in elvish, still loud enough that every elf could hear him. "Captain, any orc that continues to bear arms against us, cut them down."

"Gladly," the elf replied coolly. For a brief moment, there was a sense of anticipation, none of the orcs wanting to be the first to finally relent, the elves waiting for the signal from Zorvut, Taegan watching him in stunned awe.

The clattering sound of weapons falling to the ground broke the tense air as first one, then another, then many orcs yielded, tossing down their blades and holding up their hands in a placating gesture.

"Forward!" Kyrenic called out in elvish, brandishing his sword, and with a resounding shout the elves charged the city, racing through the streets. Only a handful of orcs stepped forward to meet them, and though they fought fiercely, they were more than outnumbered. After a brief, tense scuffle, the army of elves had cut down the few orcs who had refused to yield and continued their charge through the city to seek out any remaining rebels.

For once, Zorvut was thankful for the rigid codes and customs of orc tradition. He had slain the warlord with his own hands, and now he held command. All but the most stubborn of fighters, the absolute most disdainful of him, would not dare to continue bearing arms against him now.

He felt a trickle of tentative hope coming from the bond, and he looked toward Taegan. The elf was still crouched in the same spot, motionless, his mouth agape but the corners upturned in a hesitant smile. He was so small, so fragile, compared to the orcs that towered over him even from paces away. Guilt wracked him at the sight of reddened, blistered skin on his arm under the tatters of one of his sleeves.

He dropped his sword and stumbled toward Taegan, every cell in his body suddenly yearning to touch him, to hold him, and he fell to his knees next to him.

"You're hurt," Taegan said weakly as Zorvut hauled him into his arms, their bodies singing in rapture the instant their skin touched. For a moment it was so overwhelming he couldn't breathe, gasping for breath as he pressed Taegan's trembling form against his own.

"I'm okay," Zorvut said softly, then pulled away to look down at him. "*You're* hurt. I'm sorry, I'm so sorry I burnt you. I had to get him away from you. He was going to kill you. I'm so sorry."

"It's okay," Taegan replied, his voice still hoarse, and he looked down at the wound. "It's okay. I'll be okay now."

Fear still radiated from the bond despite his words. Zorvut bit his lip, taking in a deep, slow breath before speaking again. "Let me get you untied."

The poor elf's wrists were bound tightly together, but with some careful placement Zorvut split the chain apart below where it was knotted, breaking his hands free. Before either could even say anything, though, Taegan lifted his freed hands and wrapped his arms around Zorvut's torso, pressing his face into his chest despite the blood and sweat smeared across his body.

"I thought—I thought—" Taegan stammered, his voice suddenly breaking with emotion. "He was going to kill you, Zorvut."

Gingerly, Zorvut returned the embrace, holding his husband close to him and closing his eyes. Everything had been worth it for this sensation, the familiar closeness, the way the world seemed to slide back into tune when they were together.

"I know," he replied softly. "But I wouldn't let him."

"I missed you," Taegan continued, his voice muffled against Zorvut's skin. "I missed you so much."

"I know," Zorvut said, his own voice starting to quiver. He had to hold it together while they were surrounded, but it was proving to be a harder task than he thought. Suddenly feeling painfully aware of so many eyes still on him, he stood up, helping Taegan stumble to his feet before carefully hugging him again. "I missed you, too."

"Your mother!" Taegan gasped, pulling back just enough to look up into Zorvut's eyes. His face was glistening, smeared with a mix of tears and blood and sweat, likely just as much of his own as Zorvut's. "She's here. They kept her in the prison across from me, but... I don't know where she is now. But I think she may still be in Drol Kuggradh somewhere."

Zorvut hesitated. Something in his heart ached at the words, but he could not quite place the feeling it elicited in him. Happiness, uncertainty, repulsion, somehow a mix of each all at once?

"You," he said in orcish, looking toward the orc standing nearest to them, who snapped to attention with an uncertain expression. "Bring me Naydi Bonebreaker from the prison, or wherever she is. Alive."

"Y-Yes," the other orc stammered, nodding quickly before striding away, leaving his weapon behind.

"Was she hurt?" Zorvut asked, looking back at Taegan.

"Well, yes," Taegan said, glancing over the way the guard had gone. "She... We had tried to escape, but they caught her, and broke her arm and hauled her away."

"Are you hurt?" he asked, abruptly pushing Taegan back to look more closely at him. Other than the burn and bloody nose, he looked alright, but if they had tried to escape... "Did they hurt you at all?"

Taegan grimaced, shaking his head. "No, nothing like that. Hrul threatened me, pushed me around a bit, but... Mostly I'm just hungry." He grinned weakly, as if trying to laugh but unable to produce the sound. "You're the one who's hurt. Look at you." He touched Zorvut's arm lightly where it was cut open, the gash sticky with drying blood. He could feel the tightness in Taegan's chest as if it were his own, the relief and despair welling up all at once. "Zorvut, I'm so sorry. I'm sorry you had to do all this for me. Back in Naimere, I should have just listened to you. I shouldn't have been out in the taverns and talking to people... This is my fault."

"No," Zorvut snapped, grabbing Taegan's hand on his arm quickly. The elf looked up at him, startled, tears glistening in his eyes but not quite falling. "No, don't say that. This wasn't your fault. It was—" He scowled at the sudden thought and looked around. "Kelvhan—where is he?"

"Dead," Taegan answered, and Zorvut raised an eyebrow, surprised. "Hrul killed him pretty much the moment we arrived. I don't think he ever planned to uphold whatever bargain they had struck... And I think Kelvhan would have seen that if he wasn't so blinded by wanting revenge."

Zorvut frowned, but nodded slowly. One less thing for him to worry about, he supposed, though it should not surprise him to hear that Hrul had turned against the only elf that would want to work with him. He couldn't pretend to understand what must have been going through either of their heads.

"I'm just relieved you're safe," he said softly once the information had sunk in. "I know it seems silly, since I'm sure I would have felt it, but the whole time I was afraid that I... That I might come here to find you dead. I don't know what I would have done."

"He wanted you to have to watch," Taegan said darkly. His eyes slipped away from Zorvut's gaze, focusing down on the burnt, dead orc on the ground for a long moment. "He said he would kill me in front of you, then kill you."

"He's dead now," Zorvut said, and though he felt some guilt as he said it, it was not nearly as much as he might have expected to feel. "We don't have to worry about this ever again."

"Zorvut!" a voice called out in orcish, and Zorvut looked up to see the orc he had sent off had returned. Naydi followed him, shielding her eyes from the sun with one hand, the other arm bandaged and cradled close to her body.

She looked just as dirty and disheveled as Taegan, but with an emaciated thinness about her face that had not quite sunk into Taegan's, and one of her tusks was missing. The remnants of bruising and what looked like a black eye were still visible on her face. Her thin frame showed how long she must have been imprisoned, and it wracked him with guilt to see his mother in such a state.

"Zorvut?" she asked hesitantly, glancing around. When her eyes found the severed head of Hrul on the ground behind him, the dead body further beyond, she stopped in her tracks and stared, motionless.

"Mother," he said slowly in orcish, stepping closer to her—Taegan followed, and Zorvut could feel his reluctance to be any further from him than absolutely necessary. "I'm glad to see you're still alive."

"You killed him," she whispered, her eyes still locked on the corpse behind them. Finally, after an uncomfortable silence, she looked back over at him, her brows furrowed. "It was you, right?"

"Yes," he said with a nod, and understanding dawned in her eyes. "I'm freeing you from whatever sentence or judgment he passed on you. I will do what I can to keep you safe here, but... If you want to leave, I won't stop you, and I'll make sure you have enough to get started somewhere else."

Her mouth tensed into a hard line around her tusk, her conflicted emotions apparent on her face. That was understandable to him—looking down at her elicited more than a few mixed feelings in Zorvut as well. Part of him despaired at the thought of sending her away, a childlike instinct wanting the comfort of his mother near him. But another part of him burned with anger toward her, how she had lied his whole life, had endangered both his and Taegan's safety. She had let him enter the peace treaty knowing full well that if anyone discovered her secret, it could topple both nations back into war, and that was exactly what had happened. While she could not have known how her decision would have affected things when it occurred, that resentful part of him still wanted to lay the blame at her feet, regardless of whether she deserved it or not.

"I'll go," she said softly after considering for a moment. "I know there's no place for me here. So I'll go."

"Let me give you this, then," Zorvut sighed, not surprised at her choice. From his belt, he pulled his coin purse, handing her the whole pouch. He wasn't sure exactly how much was in it, but it would be more than enough for her to travel anywhere in the orcish territories and find a comfortable place to lie low for now, maybe forever. He could feel Taegan's eyes on him, curious but unsure of the meaning of their exchange. "It's for you. You shouldn't tell anyone who you are, and you should never come back here."

Finally, emotion seemed to cross her face as she squinted, fighting to hold back tears. After a moment of hesitation, she took the coin purse from his outstretched hand, first grasping his fingers with unexpected tenderness.

"I'm sorry," she said, barely above a whisper. "I never meant for any of this to happen. Please believe me. I understand if you don't want to see me again, but... I *am* sorry."

Zorvut pursed his lips, glancing away. "I know," he replied faintly. He could understand it, he thought, as much as it pained him. "You should go."

She looked aside before he could see her cry, nodding. "Yes," she agreed, and turned to leave. "Goodbye, my son." She glanced at Taegan as she stepped away, looked between them for a brief moment, then simply bowed her head toward the elf in acknowledgment before pushing her way through the crowd and disappearing.

"What just happened?" Taegan asked with a frown, watching her go. Zorvut sighed.

"She's free now, but it wouldn't be safe for her here," he said slowly, switching back to elvish. "When power passes to the next warlord, often their whole family is slain along with them. Even though she's my mother, there's no place for the former warlord's wife when the next one ascends."

Taegan seemed to consider it for a moment, then he could practically feel the realization click into place as the elf swiveled his head to look up at him, eyes wide.

"That's you, isn't it?" he asked, the shock in his voice taking Zorvut by surprise. "You killed him, so now you're...?"

Zorvut let out a bitter laugh. Somehow, it seemed, he kept ending up with power he had never asked for. "Yes, that's correct. That would make me the new warlord now."

CHAPTER ELEVEN
TAEGAN

The rest of the day passed in a blurry whirlwind. Taegan could barely keep track of the events as they happened—between the invasion of elves quashing the last of any rebellion against Zorvut, to the spreading news of Hrul's violent end and Zorvut seizing power throughout the city and beyond, there was hardly a moment for them to stop and breathe until well past nightfall.

"Where are we even going to sleep?" he asked in despair, realizing it had been several hours since sundown. Food had been brought to them, but they were sitting in the town square, where Zorvut had moved to speak with some of the other leaders in the city. Countless orc generals and soldiers had filtered in and out to arrange spreading the news of his ascension and his decree of ending the war.

"The warlord's tent," Zorvut sighed, looking over at him. His wounds had been briefly checked over and quickly cleaned up by a shaman, who had inspected and bandaged Taegan's burned arm as well, but they were both still dirty and bloody, and Taegan could feel bone-deep weariness emanating from him. "I asked to have it cleared out as much as possible, so we should be able to sleep there tonight. For the long term, I'll figure something else out. I don't think we'll be here much longer, but I can have someone take you there if you want to go lay down."

"No," Taegan replied, hardly letting Zorvut finish his sentence. "No, I'm staying with you." The half-orc gave him a wry smile.

"I won't be much longer, I promise," he murmured, leaning down to gingerly kiss Taegan's forehead. "I don't think anyone else is going to come to speak with me, but I just want to make sure everyone who wanted to has the chance."

Taegan nodded, though he felt restless and anxious to go. He had understood little of what had happened, since it was mainly orcs speaking orcish who had come to meet Zorvut, with a far more complicated mix of sentiments than he could understand just through their bond. Some had sounded angry, even violent, but he had never sensed any sort of fear coming from Zorvut, and nothing had escalated.

At first he had thought it was just leaders of the orcish armies who had wanted to converse with him, but he realized even common foot soldiers and non-warriors entirely were coming to speak with him as well. Zorvut had explained that he had to prove his worth to his people, and this process was customary, but Taegan did not really understand. But he waited patiently, despite the nervousness that still simmered in the back of his mind.

Finally, when it felt like it must have been near midnight, Zorvut turned to him and said softly in elvish, "I don't think I can stay awake much longer."

"Let's go," Taegan urged, putting a hand on his forearm, and this time Zorvut nodded in agreement. A few orc soldiers had maintained a semblance of a watch around him, and he spoke to them in a few harsh, guttural words before turning back to Taegan.

"They'll tell anyone else who comes to return in the morning," he said. "Let's go."

Zorvut stood, and Taegan followed. They were undisturbed as they left, and before long they were alone on the street, which worked out in their favor as Zorvut stumbled more than once as he walked. Taegan could feel his exhaustion from the bond as if it were his own. Some pain in his arm still lingered, but whatever salve the shaman had slathered on it seemed to have done the trick for now, and it only bothered him if he thought about it too long. Focusing on Zorvut's sore tiredness was somehow easier.

"Do you know how to get there?" he asked, coming up alongside Zorvut and placing his hand on his arm, partly as a gesture of comfort and partly in hopes of steadying his wobbling gait.

"Yes," Zorvut answered with a nod, blinking a few times. He steadied himself and continued walking, Taegan following him hesitantly.

Eventually they seemed to arrive, as Zorvut led him to what looked like an abandoned tent much larger than the surrounding ones and walked inside. Taegan glanced around, his brows furrowed, but it didn't seem like anyone was around—or inside, since there was no commotion as Zorvut entered the tent as if it were his own. So he pushed open the tent flaps as well and took a few steps inside.

It was dark, but Zorvut was already lighting a few candles to illuminate it. Although it was a tent, it seemed halfway a permanent fixture, with curtain-like room dividers set up to create a sitting area in the front and what seemed to be private quarters toward the back. Wooden fixtures held up the thick cloth of the tent in an amalgam of colors, ranging from deep purples and blues to vibrant yellows and oranges, too gaudy for Taegan's taste but certainly intending to convey importance and class. But the room seemed to have been sacked from what Taegan could tell—tables and chairs were upended, and any sign of personal belongings such as clothes or trinkets were entirely absent.

"Is it alright for us to be here?" he asked nervously as he looked around the room. Zorvut glanced back at him, a soft smile breaking his features.

"It's fine," he reassured him. "No one else will be using this tent, not anymore. It's technically mine now. I think whoever emptied it just decided to start clearing it out without thinking to tidy it up again." He gestured toward the back where a curtain was draped as some sort of door. "There should be a wooden tub back there, and a well out back. Do you..." He trailed off, suddenly seeming embarrassed as he looked away.

"What's wrong?" Taegan asked, frowning.

"Could you help me bring in some water?" he asked faintly, looking away. Taegan forced himself not to laugh, though a tender sort of amusement welled up in him at the question.

"Of course," he said, stepping briskly past the half-orc. "You're injured. Of course I'll help." He did not wait to see if Zorvut was following him before pushing through the cloth divider into the private section of the tent, where there seemed to be a sleeping area set up with another divider creating a bathroom in the far corner, or as much of a corner as could be made in a round tent. Peering along the walls, he found the loose area that indicated another tent flap, and opened it to step outside, where sure enough, a stone well stood just a few feet away.

He had never had to draw water from a well before, but surely it couldn't be that complicated, he thought. As he was looking over the mechanism, a wooden bucket on a rope attached to a pulley and handle, he could feel Zorvut come up behind him with a chuckle.

"You just toss it down," he said, reaching over to take the bucket from Taegan's hands. "I was just about to," he scowled, but he couldn't hold the face for long against the good-natured smile that played at the half-orc's lips. In spite of the chaotic whirlwind of the day, there was still the same comfort of just being in Zorvut's presence.

With some effort they carried in bucket after bucket until they'd filled the wooden tub, and with a flick of his wrist, Zorvut lit the fire underneath it to warm the water.

"I would invite you in with me, but..." he said, and gestured to the blood and grime that had accumulated on him. Taegan grimaced, thinking of how painful the hot water would be on his own injury.

"Maybe next time," he said, shaking his head. "But I'll help you bathe, at least."

Zorvut was visibly in pain as he lowered himself into the warm water, wincing and groaning as his wounds were washed. His torso was mottled with tender bruising, and in the light Taegan could see one of his eyes was bruised, the sclera stained with red. He looked so vulnerable, sitting there wounded and naked, that Taegan could not quite bring himself to look at his face at first, instead focusing only on the parts of his body he was gently wiping clean with a soft cloth. As tired as he was, Zorvut definitely seemed to be the worse for wear between them.

Despite his obvious discomfort, though, the half-orc was nearly nodding off in the water by the time Taegan had wiped him down, the once-clean bath now murky and reddish. The water had become tepid and cool, but the half-orc's eyes remained closed when Taegan walked away to go get him a towel, and he did not respond when he came up to the side of the wooden tub once more.

"Sorry," he groaned, as Taegan gently shook his shoulder. "I'm awake."

"Just need to get you out of here, then you can go right to bed," Taegan murmured, handing him the towel as Zorvut rose to his feet. He helped guide Zorvut to the bed, a massive orc-sized pile of blankets and cushions, so there would be more than enough room for the both of them. He crawled into the bed with some difficulty, but the moment his eyelids closed, he was asleep. Taegan draped a blanket over him and looked down at his face for a long moment, a strange mix of pride and worry and happiness and fear welling in his heart all at once.

Much as he was tired, too, a bath sounded far too alluring. There were still a few embers from the fire Zorvut had lit, so with some effort Taegan drained the wooden tub, brought up a few buckets of clean water, and stoked the fire to warm it. His own muscles ached with exertion as he had to painstakingly climb over the edge of the tub that was nearly as tall as he was and hold his arm at an awkward angle to keep his wound out of the water, but the comforting warmth soothed him. He hadn't been able to do more than wipe himself clean with cold water in the weeks—had it been weeks?—since his capture, so even the warm water alone felt decadent. After a moment's rest, though, Taegan meticulously scrubbed himself clean. Swarm water loosened the dried blood on his face and his body, although it still took some scrubbing to get rid of the feeling of sticky debris on his skin. The process was exhausting, but when he stood up from the dirty water and no longer saw a sheen of dried sweat over his skin and could finally distinguish his freckles instead of flecks of dirt and blood, relief overwhelmed him. He would never take a good bath for granted again.

He did not bother to find clean clothes when he finally managed to pull himself out of the tub and blow out the last few candles, instead burrowing under the blankets next to Zorvut, pressing their bodies close. Zorvut made a soft, sleepy sound at the intrusion, but otherwise did not stir as he came to bed.

Even as tired as he was, Taegan still felt restless and nervous for a long moment as he laid there silently in the dark. He had seen the warlord beheaded with his own eyes, yet some primal part of him still paced with fear that someone might attack them in the night, or they would kidnap him again, or worse. Was it really over?

Sleep took him eventually, but not before he'd turned the thought over in his mind again and again.

CHAPTER TWELVE
ZORVUT

When Zorvut woke the next morning, his whole body was stiff and painful. The wound on his back especially stung from how he'd been laying on it, but as he tried to sit up, every muscle and joint burned in protest. He took in a few deep breaths before forcing himself to get up, an involuntary groan escaping his lips as he did. Once he was sitting up, the pain wasn't as bad, but he still took a moment to brace himself before looking down at Taegan.

The elf was still asleep next to him, curled up in the blankets but shifted in what looked like an uncomfortable angle to keep pressure off his wounded arm. It had been bandaged when Zorvut had gone to sleep, but Taegan must have unwrapped it—the skin was red, glistening, and mottled from elbow to shoulder, and guilt filled him at the sight. Part of him knew it was far better than the alternative, that in the moment he had only done what he knew would save Taegan's life, but still he hated himself for having done it. He was thinner than Zorvut remembered, too, much of his muscle tone lost and replaced with a gauntness that betrayed how he must have suffered. And, though it was hard to see at this angle, Zorvut could just make out the edges of bruising along his throat where he had been strangled; he hadn't seen it the night before, but now in the light of the morning it was a dark and painful-looking purple.

He had to look away to keep himself from weeping then. Much as he had hoped being reunited with his husband would only be joyful, the evidence of how cruelly he had been treated, still so fresh, all but broke his heart.

"Zorvut?" Taegan's voice was small and sleepy, and as he looked back down the elf's eyes had barely slid open, peering up at him in concern. "Are you all right?"

"Yes," Zorvut replied with a nod, though his voice was rough, right on the edge of breaking. "I just... I was so worried about you. I'm sorry I hurt you."

Taegan's green eyes glanced away as he spoke, glancing over at his arm. He shifted slightly, then winced as he lifted his head.

"Is my neck bruised?" he asked, his voice sounding raspier the louder he spoke. Zorvut grimaced and nodded.

"Lift your head a little so I can see," he said, and slowly Taegan tilted his head up. Zorvut cringed at the red and purple band that spread from one end of Taegan's throat to the other. "Gods. Yes, it... that looks painful."

"It is," Taegan groaned, letting his head tip forward again. A dull pain was coursing through the bond, but it dimmed as they spoke; Taegan must have been trying to keep it stifled. "I think... Can I just stay here today? Is that alright?"

"Of course," Zorvut agreed; the prospect sounded appealing to him, too, but he knew there was too much to be done for him to hide away for the entire day. "I'll have someone bring you food and water, but stay and rest for as long as you need."

"Okay," Taegan murmured, his eyes already fluttering closed. Zorvut frowned and placed his hand against Taegan's forehead.

"You're feverish," he said, his hand resting on Taegan's face for a moment. "Do you feel sick?"

"Just hurts," he replied, not opening his eyes. "I'll sleep it off."

Zorvut nodded, letting his gaze linger on Taegan for a moment longer before he forced himself to his feet, stumbling out of the bed. He would have to send a healer to look at him, too.

With some effort, he slowly managed to dress himself and make his way out of the tent, though it was later in the morning than he had hoped when he finally emerged into the sunlight. Two elves were posted just outside, keeping watch, and looked up at him expectantly as he exited.

"Prince Taegan is still inside," he said as one stepped forward to greet him. "Make sure someone brings him food and water, and... maybe a healer to check up on him, too."

"Yes, of course," the elf agreed, nodding. He gestured toward the other, who quickly pulled their helmet back on and strode away.

Zorvut did not look back as he kept walking, making his way to the center of town and trying to mask his limping gait as best he could. He would be beholden to the rite of proving for another day, so that there would be enough time for each and every orc to come speak to him if they wanted to. It was a primarily symbolic act—Zorvut could not recall if anything anyone said during the proving had ever truly impacted the way a warlord ruled, but it at least gave the illusion of the people being heard. Maybe he could be the one to finally change things. Maybe.

When he arrived, a handful of both elves and orcs were standing watch, but the first orc he noticed, he recognized immediately.

"Gorza!" he exclaimed, a surprised grin crossing his face. His youngest sister glanced over and hesitantly returned the smile, stepping closer to him. It had been several months since he'd last seen her, and she had some new tattoos around her shoulders and neck.

"Zorvut," she said carefully as she approached, her hands open at her sides. "I'm glad you lived."

"You're brave to show up here," he said with a snort. "You're the first I've heard from."

"It's no secret I had no love for him, especially not after what he did to Mom," she replied with a disdainful glance toward the city gate, where they had fought less than a day ago. "It was only a matter of time. I'm glad it was you who took the plunge."

"Well, I'm happy to see you," he said, and extended his arm. She glanced at it before stepping closer to gingerly hug him from the side. He winced, the contact making every sore muscle in his torso ache all over again, but returned the embrace.

"Listen," she said, her voice low in his ear. "Let's talk in private when you get the chance."

He hesitated, taken aback at the words. "Of course," he agreed after a beat of silence, and as she pulled away he offered, "Tomorrow morning? I'm still figuring out where everything is, but I'm guessing the warlord's tower is still the best private meeting place."

She nodded. "I can have it cleared out for you before tomorrow."

Zorvut paused, considering. Though the only tower in the city was fairly small and had only been used as a secluded meeting space and occasional guest quarters for as long as he could remember, it might work better as a temporary home than the tent they were staying in. Certainly Taegan would find it more comfortable. It was modest, but it could be expanded to a larger residence. He would have to talk to someone about it, eventually, but clearing it out would be a good first step.

"Actually, the warlord's tower might be better for us to stay in," he said, shaking his head. "Being in Hrul's tent was, well, unsettling. Is there a different meeting place?" "We can find somewhere else," she replied, shrugging. "I'll still have it cleared out, though, if that's your plan for it." "Yes, if you could do that, I'd appreciate it," he said with a nod.

"Great. I'll get on it," she said, and smirked. "I know you're busy, so I'll stay out of your hair for now. We'll talk tomorrow." Before he could reply, she had already turned to go, and he watched her leave with a pensive frown. It certainly seemed as though Gorza was on his side, and they had always gotten along well, but for her to be so cryptic and careful with her words was not like her.

But it would be tomorrow's problem, he thought as he took his place in the town square—a line of orcs had already formed to speak with him. He sat down in the plain wooden chair that had been left for him, and gestured for the first of them to approach.

Zorvut was unsure how many orcs he ended up speaking to in the time that he sat there. It started with some he recognized, warriors who had been loyal to Hrul, who mainly asked him about his plans for the war, or rather for the peace treaty he had expressed his intention to reinstate. Most seemed unhappy that he would be ending things even after his explanations, but largely, they accepted his decree. He had killed Hrul, and they would not try to fight him, at least not openly. Not yet.

Next were soldiers, all of them unfamiliar to him. But they asked him mostly the same questions, his plans for the elves, the fighting, the other orcs. He did not have many set plans just yet, and he could tell his answers did not always satisfy their questions.

And then—a smaller figure approached him, a child, and his heart sank at the familiar face. The first messenger he'd sent ahead, the boy whose sister he'd killed. He met the boy's silent, dark gaze for a long moment until he could bring his name to the forefront of his memory.

"Vurak," he said finally, his voice low, and the boy seemed to flinch at the words but took a step closer to him. "I'm glad to see you're alive."

"You killed my sister," the boy said faintly, just loud enough for him to hear. "Our parents have been gone for a long time. I don't know where my clan is anymore.

I..." Vurak's eyes suddenly gleamed with unshed tears, and he looked away with a scowl. "I'm hungry. I don't have anywhere to live. And it's your fault. Why should I have to follow you?"

"You don't," Zorvut replied, leaning back in his chair. The boy shot him a glare, but Zorvut shook his head. "You don't. You can go back to your clan, or any other. I cannot force anyone to stay if they don't want to be here."

"How?" he spat, anger clearly overtaking him as he took another step toward Zorvut, more aggressively this time. The elf standing watch behind him took a step forward, hand on his weapon, but Zorvut lifted his own hand in a placating gesture and after a beat of hesitation, the elf backed down. "I have my horse, but nothing to feed her, nothing for me to eat. I don't have the gear to go more than a day or two away."

For the second time, Zorvut pulled his coin purse from his belt, and offered the whole thing to Vurak. It was less than what he had on him the day before, but certainly far more coin than the boy could have hoped to procure hunting or foraging. Vurak stared silently at it for a moment, his angry yellow eyes flickering between Zorvut's unmoving face and the bag of coin.

"Take it," Zorvut said. "It should be more than enough for food, shelter. You can get everything you need to travel to another clan."

Vurak moved to snatch it from Zorvut's hand, but he kept his grip on it, the boy's eyes flashing with anger again. But Zorvut pulled him closer, their eyes meeting.

"Listen," he said. The boy's face twitched with consternation, but he didn't look away. "I'm sorry. About your sister. It was not her or your clan I wanted to fight, or anyone other than Hrul. I'm sorry it happened this way, but I want to change things, to make it so nothing like this ever happens again. Can you understand that?"

The boy's face twisted, and when he wrenched on the coin purse again, Zorvut let it go.

"I don't care if you're sorry," he spat, tears finally spilling from his eyes as he backed away. "I hate you." With that, he turned and ran. Zorvut sighed, pressing his hands to his face as the magnitude of the boy's words settled onto his shoulders. Some rational part of him knew that of course not every orc would be on his side, that of course those he had to cut down to get here would hold a grudge—still, it was an uncomfortable realization to know he would carry the weight of that guilt forever. He took in a few deep breaths, then tried to push the thought from his mind as he gestured for the next orc to approach him.

After that, it was mostly other common folk who came to him, traders and hunters and nomads. The wealthiest merchants had already come to him the day before, those who employed others and had large caravans to worry about. These were more lay folk, eking out a living with their trade to varying degrees of success. Their questions were a bit easier—if he planned any changes to their roads and villages, if trade with the elves might be a possibility—and had some small measure of hope to them. He knew the ones who had no stake or say in the battles would be willing to follow just about anyone if it meant they would be safe and their way of life would be largely unaffected. His answers to those were more hopeful as well, and more of them walked away satisfied.

All throughout the day, he could feel Taegan in the back of his head, a comforting presence after so long with silence. He slept all morning and much of the afternoon, so the sensation was muted and quiet, but the occasional flashes of emotion were enough to cause him to stifle a smile each time he felt them. Knowing Taegan was so close made the miserable day bearable.

Eventually, the crowd thinned and no more orcs approached him, though he lingered in the town square for a little while afterward just in case. But it was getting late in the afternoon now, and the next orc that greeted him was a warrior he had already spoken with.

"Warlord," he said, lowering his head respectfully. It still gave Zorvut a nervous thrill to hear the word directed toward him. "Your sister Gorza has asked me to pass a message along to you. We have largely cleared the northern tower out and it will be suitable for you to move in tomorrow. Additionally, we have received confirmation from all but the remote mountain clans that they've received word of the change of power, and all forces should pull out of Aefraya by tomorrow."

"I'm glad to hear it," Zorvut sighed, nodding as the orc spoke to him. "Nilud, right?"

"Yes, sir," the orc replied with a nod.

"Nilud, I have a task for you. I want to talk with all the generals currently in the city. Tell them I'm having a meeting tomorrow in..." He paused, considering. If they were taking up residence, however temporary, in the tower, he would have to designate a different meeting place.

Nilud seemed to sense his uncertainty, and offered, "There is a tent Hrul used as something of a war room along the western edge of town. That might be suitable. Sir."

Zorvut grimaced, but nodded. "An excellent suggestion. Yes, please tell them to meet me there before sunset. There should be five, yes?"

"Yes," Nilud agreed. "I will alert them now." He nodded stiffly, and when Zorvut waved him away, he turned and headed down an eastern street.

He was exhausted, and no one else was waiting on him, so with a few words to the elves who had been standing guard near him, he headed back toward the tent. Taegan was still in bed when he arrived, but was awake and sat up with a grin as he entered.

"I've missed you," he said, holding one arm out, and with a soft smile Zorvut came to sit next to him and gently hugged him. His wound was bandaged now, but he was still careful to avoid it. "How are you feeling?"

"Sore," Zorvut admitted with a sigh. "But I should be asking you that. Are you alright? You've slept all day."

"I'm feeling better now," Taegan said. "One of the healers came to see me. Did you send him?"

"I did," he laughed, nodding. "I'm glad that helped. I was worried about you. You were feverish this morning."

Taegan nodded, glancing down at his bandaged arm. "The healer cleaned me up and gave me a salve to apply. I should be alright now." He leaned closer to Zorvut, pressing their bodies together, sending soft comfort flowing through the bond. There was a heat behind it that Zorvut recognized, but a hesitance along with it.

"Do you...?" he asked uncertainly, looking down at Taegan's face. The elf flushed and looked away before shaking his head.

"I mean, I do want to," he stammered. "But I'm also... I don't know. Neither of us are feeling very well, so maybe it would be best to wait a little longer."

"No one hurt you, right?" Zorvut asked, fear suddenly gripping him. If something had happened, he was sure Taegan would have told him, but... "No one—no one forced you to do anything, or...?"

"No, no! Nothing like that," Taegan exclaimed, even more embarrassed now. "No, you don't need to be worried about that. I'm really just feeling under the weather still, and you're still injured."

"I understand," Zorvut answered, feeling his face flush as well. "You're right. I just was worried for a moment there." They sat in an awkward silence for a beat, both uncertain, until Zorvut blurted, "There's a tower on the north end of town. I'm having it cleared out so we can move there as more of a permanent home. It's no castle, but..."

A warm smile spread across Taegan's face, echoed by a soft fondness through the bond.

"That sounds nice. Better than a tent, to be sure," he said. "Oh—I was up and about for a bit earlier, so I wrote my father a letter. I'm assuming you had been in contact with him for you to have brought all these elves with you, but I wanted him to know we're both alright."

"I've already sent my orders to have the orcs pull out of Aefraya, but I'm sure he'll be glad to hear from you," Zorvut replied, squeezing Taegan's hand before pursing his lips in thought. "In fact... It might be best if you go back to Aefraya once you're feeling up to travel."

"Absolutely not!" Taegan protested immediately, his head snapping up toward Zorvut in surprise. "No, not after all this. I'm staying with you."

"I figured you would say that," Zorvut said with a grimace. "I don't want you to go, either, but it would probably be safer for you there. Things are bound to be... tumultuous here for a while, and your presence here could make you a target."

"I don't care," Taegan said resolutely, shaking his head. From the tone of his voice, Zorvut knew that to argue with him would be pointless, and his heart swelled with affection. This was more like the Taegan he knew. "I'll stay out of the public eye, or I'll make sure I'm with you if I have to go out. But I'm not going to leave, not after being apart for so long."

Despite the worry that lingered in the back of his head, Zorvut found himself smirking. "Well... Good. I want to be here with you, too."

"Then it's settled. I'm staying," Taegan replied decisively. Zorvut pulled him closer, hugging him carefully to his chest. Taegan's uninjured arm wrapped around his torso to return the embrace, equally cautious.

"You're staying," he agreed. When they were this close, the scent of his hair, his skin, was nearly overwhelming. "You're staying here with me."

When Zorvut left the next morning, Taegan was up and about but still hesitant to leave their shelter, so stayed behind another day.

"We'll move over to the tower tonight," Zorvut said before he left. "Since we don't have many personal belongings with us, it should be a simple process."

"I'll gather up what we want to take with us, at least," Taegan answered with a shrug, gesturing around the room. Nothing in the tent was really theirs, but it had its use all the same.

A groan escaped his lips as he stood and stretched, his bruised body protesting the movement.

"You should really take some time to rest, so you can heal," Taegan said, watching him with a concerned frown. He would certainly like to, Zorvut thought, but he shook his head.

"Too much to do," he sighed. "Maybe in a few days, everything will calm down a bit. But for now, I have to go talk to my sister."

Then he had gone to the tent he and Gorza had agreed to meet at, followed by two elven guards who kept watch outside. The tent was vacant when he opened the flap to peek in, so he stepped inside and sat down in one of the chairs that were pushed up against a long wooden table, which took up the bulk of the space.

A large world map was spread across the table, with a pile of markers pushed to one corner that Zorvut imagined must have been carefully placed along the map not so long ago. There was an unused weapons rack near the entrance, and a few tall lanterns spread around the room, but other than those, the tent was quite sparse. Whether it had always been so empty or if it had been cleared out of all but the necessities like so many other facilities Hrul had kept, he could not say.

He was not alone with his thoughts for long, though, as the tent flap burst open suddenly and Gorza entered with an almost exaggerated swagger. A scowl was on her face, but her eyes were glancing back at the elves that must have been standing guard outside the tent, and she was muttering under her breath.

"Everything alright?" he asked, lifting an eyebrow. She rolled her eyes and sat down across from him.

"Yes. The elves didn't recognize me at first. Tried to give me a hard time," she grumbled. She took in a long, slow breath as if to steady herself, and when she looked back at Zorvut, the irritated expression that had just been on her face was gone, replaced with a carefully neutral one. "Thank you for having us speak in private."

"Of course. What did you want to talk to me about?"

"Well, it's not very good news," she said bluntly. "I'm sure you've already suspected this, but there is probably going to be more fighting in the near future.

There have already been people talking about a group getting together to try and either challenge you or leave. I'm hoping they'll decide to leave. But I've heard both stories, and I don't think it's coming from two different groups."

"Hmm," Zorvut replied with a sigh. His sister was not one to beat around the bush, but he wasn't sure how much he appreciated her forthrightness in this case. "That is bad news. Have you gotten any names?"

"A few," Gorza said. "I'm keeping an eye on them. So far it seems like just talk, but you know how these things can go."

"And you're certain? How do you know this?"

At that, an amused grin spread around Gorza's tusks. "Oh, you know me," she said with a nonchalant shrug. "Gorza the Silver-tongued gets along with everyone. I've made a lot of connections. Mother would berate me for being undisciplined, but I figure if you know the right person for the job, that's one less thing you have to do yourself. So I know whose ears are to the ground, and I know who's reliable."

Zorvut stared at her for a long moment, then snorted with laughter. It was true their mother had hassled her for her outgoing nature and proclivity for parties and revelry in the past, but it was those same qualities that made her a friend to everyone, providing the personal connections he was so apparently lacking. Her presence could not be more ideal. When he laughed, it was part surprise and part relief, but Gorza's expression became decidedly unamused in response.

"Sorry, sorry," he said, shaking his head. "I'm just, well, surprised, but also very glad. I would have been happy to have you on my side regardless, but it sounds like you're exactly the person I needed."

His words seemed to assuage her, and she chuckled in response. "Well, you definitely needed someone on your side with all this. Have you heard from anyone else at all? I know Zesh was on a hunting trip and Velda was visiting another clan, but I haven't heard from any of the others."

"No," Zorvut sighed. He had been trying not to think about that. His other siblings' silence couldn't bode well; at best, it could be entirely neutral, but at worst... "No, no one's reached out to me like you have. But... With everything that happened with Mother, I'm sure everyone is having rather mixed feelings about the situation. I certainly have. To me, it seems the best-case scenario would be if they quietly left to join up with the other clans if they really can't stand me, but I don't think I should bet on that happening."

"No, I don't expect so, either," Gorza agreed. "I'll ask around about them, too. I wouldn't be surprised if Velda ends up staying with the mountain clan; I think she had her eye on a man from there she met on a hunt last summer. This might just be the excuse she needs to marry into a different clan. And Zesh..." She frowned, glancing away. Their fiery eldest brother, who had been given the moniker of Vicious the day he became an adult, needed no explanation. "Well, we both know Zesh is a loose cannon. If anyone's going to put up a fight about this, it's him."

"And of course he's away when all this happens," Zorvut sighed. He certainly didn't disagree. As the eldest, Zesh would have had the best standing to become warlord next, though orc customs made no guarantee that the firstborn child would inherit power the way the elves' did. Plus, he and Zesh had never gotten along, and he could easily see his brother harboring resentment toward him for killing the warlord and picking up the mantle that Zesh very well might have viewed as his for the taking. "Well, I don't know how far your connections may reach, but if you can keep an eye out for Zesh, too, that would be ideal."

"I'll do what I can. I know he was riding east when he left, but who knows if he's even heard the news yet? We can at least have a scout keep an eye on the wilderness roads out there. But I don't know what more we can do that far out," Gorza answered. He had no reply to that, so they sat quietly for a beat, each considering what the silence from their siblings might mean.

"Really, Gorza, thank you," Zorvut finally said after a moment, glancing up to meet her gaze. "I don't know what I'd do without someone like you here to help me. I definitely wouldn't be able to keep as close an eye on everything on my own. I owe you much."

A self-satisfied grin crept across Gorza's face, stretching her lips taught around her tusks, but when she replied, her voice had a similar softness to his own.

"I know. That's what family's for. You don't have to thank me." She reached over to squeeze his shoulder, then stood. "So when am I going to meet this elf of yours? I said maybe all of two words to him at your wedding, but I don't think he understood me. My elvish isn't as good as yours."

Zorvut laughed at that. "Soon, hopefully. He was feeling better today, and we're going to move over to the tower so he should be more comfortable. Once he's up to checking everything out, he'll be staying close to me. I know it's dangerous, and I thought of sending him back to Aefraya, but... I don't know. All of this happened because we were apart. It seems silly to leave each other now, even if he would be safer in his home."

Gorza studied his face for a long moment, and he shifted uncomfortably under her stare. Finally, she spoke as if making an announcement, "You really love this elf."

Zorvut's c flushed with heat at that, and he glanced away. "Of course I do," he muttered, feeling all at once embarrassed and strangely proud. "None of this would have happened if we didn't care for each other."

A smug grin had spread across her face as he spoke, and he wondered how it had come to this, that his baby sister was the one teasing him, the warlord, for being married.

"Gross," was all she said, and Zorvut couldn't help but laugh at the absurdity of it. "Well, that's all I wanted to talk to you about. I'll let you get back to whatever important business you have, and I'll keep you updated once I have any news."

"Thank you," he repeated, but she had already stood and was halfway out of the tent. He watched the tent flap swing closed behind her for a long moment, running their conversation over in his mind, until finally he, too, stood up with a sigh. He still had much to do today, meetings with generals and merchants, not to mention dealing with moving Taegan to the northern tower, and still his wounds ached in protest every time he moved. Soon, maybe, he could rest, but he wouldn't hold his breath.

Chapter Thirteen

Taegan

After almost a full day of uninterrupted sleep, Taegan was feeling far better than he expected to. He had slept away most of the time he had been in captivity, but something about sleeping in an actual bed with no threat of danger looming over him was so much more restful. The burn on his arm still stung but was healing without issue. And he still felt weak—and looked it, too, seeing the gauntness of his face in the mirror as he dressed. But all things considered, he thought he was doing quite well.

Zorvut, though—he could sense the poor half-orc's exhaustion in the back of his mind all day, a constant, steady stream of yearning to rest but knowing he could not. Taegan knew times were tenuous and Zorvut could not afford to shirk his new responsibilities long enough to take a break, but still it pained him to feel how tired his husband was from the very moment he woke up.

After Zorvut had left that morning, Taegan idly bathed and dressed before gathering the things he thought they'd like to bring with them to their new lodgings. He had no personal belongings here, of course, and Zorvut only had a handful. Most of what they had was already in the tent when they arrived—it made Taegan's skin crawl to think of them as Hrul's belongings, but that was what they were—or had been provided to them over the course of the last two days. There wasn't much he thought they would need to take, but he gathered up some blankets, the clothes some of the other elves had given him, Zorvut's clothes, and a few books he had scavenged. Then he bundled them up and waited for Zorvut to return.

It was late in the afternoon when the tent flap swung open and Zorvut stepped inside, Taegan looking up from where he had been sitting on the bed with a book. There had not been much else to do, and a grin spread across his face at the sight of his husband.

"Welcome back," he said, getting to his feet. Zorvut smiled at him, reaching out to take his hand. The steady trickle of weariness in the back of his head seemed to fade a bit as they embraced, and Zorvut held onto him from a long moment, as if the contact of their skin alone could replenish him, before finally pulling away to meet his eyes.

"Ready?" he asked, and Taegan nodded. "I'll take you there."

They left the tent hand in hand, and although Taegan was quite aware of the two elven soldiers following them at a polite distance, it felt almost like a leisurely stroll through the city the way they would often walk together through the castle grounds and gardens in Aefraya. Not quite, but almost.

"This is where we'll stay," Zorvut said, pointing toward a tall building as they approached. It was a stone tower, a bit narrow and no more than three stories from what Taegan could tell, plain and unassuming. "This used to be where the warlord or some other honored guest would stay whenever they were in Drol Kuggradh, although I think Hrul had been using it as a meeting place most recently. Since I don't plan on roving much, I'm going to have it modified somewhat to work better as a permanent home, but it'll still do for now."

"As long as it's got a bath, I can't complain," Taegan teased, and Zorvut smirked down at him.

"I had one brought in just for you," he murmured, squeezing his shoulder. "Only the best for my prince."

The soft tone of Zorvut's words in juxtaposition with the strong musculature of his body pressed against Taegan made him hard almost instantly; it had been long enough that it didn't take much, but today he was feeling far more capable of that sort of physical activity compared to how lethargic he had been yesterday. Taegan knew his desire must have come loud and clear through the bond, but still he glanced away coyly, studying the stone tower for a moment longer before looking back up at Zorvut.

"Let me show you inside," Zorvut said softly, the familiar heat of his gaze setting Taegan's whole body alight. He nodded quickly, and Zorvut led him to the doorway of the tower.

They stepped inside, but the moment the door had closed behind them, Zorvut pulled him into his arms, lifting him up to kiss him hard on the mouth as Taegan's hands fumbled with the laces of his shirt. Arousal arced between them from the bond, building up rapidly to an irresistible ache between his legs that he could feel readily mirrored from Zorvut.

"Is this okay?" Zorvut asked, breaking the kiss abruptly to look down at him. "I don't want to—I know you weren't feeling well. Are you sure this is alright?"

"Yes," Taegan said, nodding firmly. "Yes, I'm sure." He tilted his head up once more expectantly, and with a slight chuckle Zorvut kissed him again. Taegan's hands pushed under Zorvut's shirt, feeling the hard muscle underneath, gingerly brushing around the places he could feel were tender and healing, tracing along the soft mound of his nipples until they grew hard under his touch. He whimpered as Zorvut mirrored the movement, his hands moving urgently under Taegan's shirt and leaving trails of warm, tingling pleasure along his skin where he touched.

"I need to be inside you," Zorvut gasped as he pulled Taegan's shirt off him, pushing him up against the stone wall just within the tower. Taegan barely took in any of their surroundings—stone walls, a hallway, maybe a table in the corner?—but all he could focus on was the heat radiating from every inch of his skin that Zorvut touched and the insistent need pulsing from the back of his head in time with his pounding heart.

"Please," Taegan whimpered, nodding quickly. He unlaced his breeches and Zorvut pulled them down in one quick, easy motion. His cock sprang free, but Zorvut's hands went straight for his ass, spreading him apart and running his fingers along Taegan's hole already wet with slick. He moaned as Zorvut pushed a finger inside of him, moving slowly but intently. It had been so long since they were last together, making the sensation somehow familiar yet new all at once. He clung desperately to Zorvut's neck, his arms quivering, but the half-orc had him held firmly in one arm with his back pressed to the wall, and with his legs wrapped around Zorvut's waist he could feel his rock-hard erection pressed against him even through the cloth of Zorvut's breeches that still separated them.

"You're so tight," Zorvut murmured as he worked his fingers in and out of Taegan, eliciting a string of soft moans and gasps from him as he did. "Gods, you're going to feel so good around me." A second finger pressed inside him, and Taegan's head tipped back against the stone wall as a soft keen escaped his lips.

"Please," he gasped, but he couldn't bring himself to formulate any words beyond that. "Please, Zorvut, please."

Zorvut worked him open for a moment longer, but the desire and pleasure building up between them proved to be too much to resist. He pulled his hand away, leaving Taegan empty only for a moment as he unlaced his own trousers, and pressed the head of his cock into Taegan's entrance.

They both gasped as his cock slid in, stretching Taegan wide and opening his body up for what felt like the first time all over again. The fullness of him, familiar as it was, overwhelmed him quickly, and he found himself pressing his face into Zorvut's shoulder and digging his fingernails frantically into his back.

"Slow," he begged, his whole body burning with heat. "You're so big—please—go slow."

"I will," Zorvut murmured. Taegan could feel him nod, and one of his hands came up to stroke Taegan's hair in a comforting gesture. "I won't hurt you."

His hips moved slowly at first as Taegan's muscles and nerves re-acclimated to the massive cock inside him, but even through the discomfort Taegan could feel the familiar building tension in his own cock with every careful thrust.

"I'm close," he moaned, squeezing his eyes shut against the pleasure that burned white-hot in the back of his head.

"I want to feel you," Zorvut murmured encouragingly, his pace as steady as ever. "I want to feel you come on me."

"I'm coming," he gasped, the words sending him over the edge. His body clenched around Zorvut's cock in time with each thrust as he shot thick streams of come onto his chest and Zorvut's abs. Everything went white for one intense moment, Zorvut's soft voice in his ear finally bringing him back to the earth.

"I feel you, gods, I feel you still coming," the half-orc was moaning against him, thrusting into him faster as a desperate tone tinged his voice. "You're so good, fuck, you feel so good..."

Taegan nodded wordlessly, only able to cling to Zorvut as he was fucked, Zorvut's hips moving quicker now of their own accord. Through the bond he could feel how close he was, the pleasure arcing between them as if it were his own cock surrounded by tight wetness. He was spent, but his hypersensitive body reacted in kind, and he bit into Zorvut's shoulder as he felt the half-orc come, driving him over the edge again. His hole clenched and pulsed around his cock as he was pumped full, hot streams of come overflowing out of him and spilling to the ground.

"I love you," he whimpered, trembling as Zorvut gasped and moaned in his ear. "I love you. I missed you so much."

After a long moment, both of them panting to catch their breath, Zorvut pulled back a bit so Taegan was not pressed against the wall and instead only braced against the half-orc's waist and chest, his arms wrapped around him tightly.

"I love you too," he said, his voice gravelly but with a comfortable sense of satisfaction radiating from the bond.

"We really made a mess," Taegan chuckled, glancing down at the pile of clothes at their feet and the puddle of come underneath him.

"I'm only a bit sorry," Zorvut replied, following his gaze. "I'll carry you to the bathroom and then we can finish the tour?"

Once they were there, Zorvut carefully set him down and drew a bucket of warm water for him to wash with.

"I'll go deal with the mess downstairs," he said with a resigned sigh after quickly wiping himself down with a wet cloth, and Taegan watched him leave still in the nude with a slight laugh. It was good to know they were truly alone here, at least.

Taegan cleaned off to the best of his ability without entirely taking a bath, though the prospect was tempting. But Zorvut had promised him a tour of what was to be his new home, so instead he found a soft, silky robe hanging on the door and wrapped himself in it before padding barefoot back down the stone stairs to find him again.

"It's not quite a castle," Zorvut said with a chagrined expression once they were back at the top level of the three-story tower, where their sleeping chamber was. "But it's comfortable."

"I don't need a castle," Taegan chuckled, shaking his head. "And this is perfectly fine."

That was the truth—while it was a far cry from the castle in Aefraya, it was still a comfortable living space with all the amenities he might need. The first floor housed a small kitchen, dining area, and common room with several different comfy chairs and tables, clearly meant for visitors to gather and socialize. The second floor had a small bathroom and another common area, though this room seemed to have more storage and was less inviting overall. Finally, the third floor was their bedroom and private bath, and had little in the way of decoration but the soft plush bed and luxurious sheets made up for the austerity of the rest of it.

"I wanted to get rid of as much as I could that belonged to my—to Hrul," Zorvut said, correcting himself quickly as he watched Taegan peering around the bare walls of the room, envisioning where to put their things. "I want this to be my space. Our space. I don't want to think about him at all, you know?"

"I understand," Taegan said with a nod. "If it helps, I don't see any sign of him here at all. We can make all this our own."

Zorvut smiled over at him, but he could still feel some lingering uncertainty from the bond. Taegan stepped closer to him, wrapping his arms around his waist to look up at his face.

"You're nervous," he said softly. "What's wrong?"

Zorvut hesitated, glancing away. "I'm glad you're here, but it is still dangerous. And my sister, Gorza, was just telling me this morning that she's heard some whispers of a group possibly trying to seize power. Your presence here could be... an additional motivation for them to act."

He looked back down at Taegan once more, his brows furrowed. "The vast majority of the orcs I've spoken with, those who aren't involved in the fighting or are merchants that operate out of Drol Kuggradh... They aren't opposed to me, or even to the idea of unification with the elves. They only want a safe environment to live their lives. It's just a small group of warriors, soldiers, that still have some loyalty to Hrul or some objection to me, as a half-orc, or you as my husband and the elves as a whole... Those are the only ones that may cause trouble, but they have the power to cause a lot of it."

"I won't leave your side," Taegan said quickly. "No one will even have a chance to harm me."

"Well," Zorvut replied with a grimace. "That will be safest. But I'm also worried about everyone else in the city. If fighting breaks out, they may catch innocents in the crossfire. They're all my responsibility now."

"Very noble of you," Taegan said with a sly grin, squeezing him a bit tighter. "You sound truly kingly now. Or, warlordy, I suppose."

"About that," Zorvut said, answering with a slight smile of his own. "I think that if we do succeed in unifying the orc wildlands with Aefraya, the power structure should change accordingly. I don't know how well it will go over with the orcs, but I think establishing a monarchy rather than this feudal warlord system... It could create a lot of stability. I mean, we would need at least a few clans to be on board, and I'm sure some won't want to join, but... I expect a number of them are ready to move toward a less tumultuous lifestyle."

Taegan paused, mulling over the proposition. Part of him balked at the idea of orcs accepting a monarchy, considering how nebulous and violent their existing power structure was—but if Zorvut truly thought that times had changed and the majority were in favor of something else, who was he to argue?

"That will be difficult," he replied slowly. "But you know I'm on your side. No matter what you decide, you have my support."

A faint grin spread around Zorvut's tusks as he squeezed Taegan a bit tighter. "I appreciate that. I know it'll be an uphill battle, but I think it will benefit everyone in the end. It's just a matter of convincing everyone else of that."

"You mentioned your sister," Taegan said. "You think she's trustworthy? Have any of your other siblings reached out to you?"

"I trust her," Zorvut replied firmly, quickly enough that Taegan had no doubt of it. "She's the only one who has been in contact with me, though. It seems like the others were not in the city when everything happened, and... Well, I suspect they aren't happy about me taking the title of warlord. So they may have gone to join a different clan, or... I don't know. I'm hoping they're not part of whatever group is considering trying to overthrow me, but I can't discount it entirely."

"Hmm," Taegan murmured. That would certainly be a disappointment, but he didn't know Zorvut's family well enough to guess one way or another. And something from the bond felt guarded, like Zorvut had more thoughts on the matter he did not want Taegan to know of. "Well, what do you know of this group, then?"

"Very little," he replied with a grimace. "Gorza has been the one with her hand on the pulse of it all, so to speak. She's always been very social and has contacts in nearly every group in the city, official or not. But even she has only really been able to give me bits and pieces. Whoever these orcs are, they know enough to keep their conversations to themselves. It's good they know their sentiment isn't likely to be well-received as a whole, but it's concerning in its own way. The less we know, the less we will be able to prepare."

"How about from the elves you've brought with you? Have you heard from them about orcs giving them trouble or anything like that?" he asked.

Zorvut paused, thinking. Taegan could practically feel the gears ticking in his head like clockwork as he must have been running through all the conversations he'd had with them in the past days.

"No," he said slowly. "I don't think so. But I will speak with the captain to be certain everything gets reported, no matter how small. They know I have some concern, but I'll make sure that's reiterated."

"Hopefully my presence here will help at least a bit, although I'm sure they've given you no trouble so far," he said, and Zorvut smirked at that.

"No. I wouldn't have made it without them," he said. A flicker of protectiveness burned through the bond, taking Taegan by surprise. "It reminds me of a conversation we had once, about how elves are loyal to their monarchs because of their trust in the gods. I've found that to be true. I know some of them may still have their qualms about me, but they trust in the fact that I'm a leader and have never given me a reason to distrust them. It's... a refreshing change from dealing with orcs, to be honest. They're very different."

"I'm glad to hear that," Taegan said with a slight smile. It was indeed something he had hoped to hear, but given how every elf in the castle had seemed to walk on tiptoe around them for months when they were first married, it was a pleasant surprise.

"Anyway, all that to say, we should be cautious for the next few weeks," Zorvut continued. "If anything does happen, I'd expect it to be sooner rather than later, now. Stay close to me and we should be alright, though." A slight, dark grin spread across his face at that. "Maybe I'll finally have the chance to show off a bit of what I've learned for you."

Over the next few days, Taegan mostly stayed sequestered in the stone tower. For all his bravado, he was hesitant to be out and about in the orc city now that he was here; as strange as it was, considering he had seen almost none of Drol Kuggradh when he was held captive, it kept reminding him of the miserable days spent in the underground dungeon in the darkness, the cold. But in their shared quarters it was comfortable with a fire always going, and he could curl up in a chair or in their bed with a book, or sit at one of the windows and observe the streets in safety. Zorvut seemed to sense his uncertainty, and didn't press.

But he knew he couldn't stay in the tower forever. So after a few days, he finally traded his loungewear for something nicer as he dressed in the morning.

"Heading out with me today?" Zorvut asked, watching him dress from their bed. Taegan turned back and smiled at him.

"That's the plan," he said, holding a soft blue tunic up to his chest. "What do you think? I want to fit in."

Amusement trickled through the bond as Zorvut sat up to look at him more closely. "I don't think there will be much you can do to avoid standing out, my love. But it is a flattering color on you."

"The next best thing, then," Taegan sighed, bright green eyes peering back at himself in the mirror. He finally felt healthy again, and the sickly pale pallor was gone from his face, but the tunic was just a touch too baggy, still. At least the light blue was a flattering color on him.

When Zorvut left, Taegan was at his side, and they walked together toward the town square. Two elven soldiers followed them, not so close that they would eavesdrop, but close enough that they could keep a watchful eye on them. Taegan glanced back at them briefly, but tried not to think about their presence too hard.

"So what's your plan for the day?" he asked, leaning a bit closer to Zorvut.

"Mainly I need to talk with my sister, Gorza," he said, glancing down at Taegan with a soft fondness welling up from the bond. "I don't think you've met yet. But I'm hoping she has some more news for me about... well, I told you."

"We haven't met yet, no. I hope she has good news for you."

Doubt flickered from Zorvut, like a shadow flickering over the bond. "I hope so, too," he replied, more softly this time. Clearly, he did not feel confident he might receive any favorable news. He couldn't say anything to that, so they walked in silence the rest of the way.

Zorvut led him to one of the larger tents near the town square—he still did not quite understand why some tents appeared to be permanent fixtures, yet were not moved to some of the stone or wooden buildings around town. This tent was one of the largest, a patchwork of purple, red, and yellow cloth, similar to the warlord's tent they had stayed in the first few nights in Drol Kuggradh, and two orc guards were standing watch outside. Taegan could feel their eyes lock onto him as they approached, but neither said anything and only gave the slightest of nods toward Zorvut.

As they entered, Taegan glanced around the room quickly, noting more strangely permanent fixtures—bookshelves and display cases, a large wooden table with a map and a range of markers spread out upon it, several chairs—and, with a start, he realized one chair was inhabited. Zorvut seemed mildly surprised, as well, but did not seem concerned as he greeted the orc sitting at the far end of the table.

Again Taegan could feel the orc's eyes on him as Zorvut spoke to him in orcish, and the stranger was silent for a moment before finally he looked back to Zorvut and responded. Taegan had no idea what they were saying, but then Zorvut gestured toward him and he heard his own name somewhere in the words he spoke, so he managed a polite, tight smile in greeting. If Zorvut was not concerned, he would try not to be, either. From the bond he couldn't quite tell what the orc was saying, only that Zorvut felt exasperated and had heard the questions before.

They spoke for only a moment before the other orc left, bowing stiffly before exiting through the tent flap on the opposite side of the room.

"What was that about?" Taegan asked, his eyes lingering on the swaying tent flap.

"He's a merchant," Zorvut said with a sigh. "One that won't leave me alone. He wants updates regarding a trade route to Aefraya when I have no news. I told him you don't speak any orcish, otherwise I'm sure he would have talked your ear off, too."

Taegan chuckled at that but didn't have the chance to respond—from behind them a voice called out in orcish, muffled as if from a distance, but he glanced back anyway. After a moment the tent flap they had entered from opened once more, and another orc stepped inside, this one female and less intimidating as she was closer to Zorvut in height, but with a scowl on her face that gave Taegan pause.

"Gorza!" Zorvut exclaimed behind him, stepping up to the orc. He said something in orcish, then turned to Taegan and said in elvish, "This is my sister, Gorza, who I told you about. She knows a bit of elvish. Gorza, Taegan is joining me today."

Gorza met Taegan's gaze and hesitated for a moment before grimacing. Immediately he could tell her mind was elsewhere, and a tight knot of tension squeezed through the bond, too, hinting that Zorvut felt the same.

"Taegan," she said briskly, nodding toward him. "I'm glad to finally meet you. Unfortunately, Zorvut, I come with bad news."

Zorvut frowned. "Let's hear it."

She sighed, glancing between them, then said in a lower voice, "It's Zesh. He's gathered a group from the outlying clans, and they're marching on Drol Kuggradh."

Chapter Fourteen
TAEGAN

There was a beat of silence, then Zorvut sat down at the large table with a long, slow sigh. The bond was suddenly quiet; whatever he was feeling, he must have been tightly guarding. Taegan glanced between him and Gorza for a moment, brows furrowed.

"Zesh is... your brother, right?" he asked, tentatively breaking the nervous quietude. Gorza gave a single terse nod.

"Our eldest brother, yes," Zorvut replied slowly, running a hand over his face as he spoke. "No one had heard from him, or our sister, since I took Drol Kuggradh. But as the eldest, I suppose he may have felt... entitled, in a way, to becoming the next warlord. I'm not surprised, but it is disappointing to hear."

"And depending on the size of his army, he may have a real chance at taking Drol Kuggradh," Gorza interjected.

A flash of anger burned from the bond, but was gone by the time Taegan looked back over at Zorvut.

"I won't let that happen," he said, his voice a low growl. "No, the people of Drol Kuggradh want peace. Even if Zesh has gathered an army, we have one, too."

"It may be smaller," Gorza replied softly. "I mean, we have the elves, but... I haven't been able to figure out for sure how many orcs ride with Zesh, and I'm certain he has some sympathizers in the city. And he's not far. From what I was told, I'd expect them in a day, maybe two."

"A day?!" Taegan exclaimed, startled, and from behind him he heard Zorvut groan in frustration as well.

"You could have led with that, Gorza," he snapped, leaning over the table to study the map spread out upon it. He seemed to consider it for a moment, then looked back at her. "If he's gathered orcs from the outlying clans, he's almost certainly coming from the west. Have the guard on the western wall doubled and warn everyone to be on the alert. At the first sign of a group, they're to sound the alarm. Make sure the elves know, too."

"I'm on it," Gorza said, and she had ducked back out of the tent just as suddenly as she'd arrived.

They remained in anxious silence for a long moment, Zorvut's gaze lingering on the map as Taegan watched him uncertainly, feeling a muffled range of emotions from the bond that he could not quite identify.

After a moment Zorvut finally looked back over at him, his lips pressed together in a tight line around his tusks.

"Come here," he said softly, gesturing for Taegan to step closer to him. He obliged, and the half-orc took him into his arms, hugging him tightly as Taegan let out a surprised, nervous laugh.

"Maybe I should have gone back to Aefraya after all, like you said," he sighed, returning the embrace. Even sitting, Zorvut had to lower his head to press his face into Taegan's shoulder. He could feel him take in a few long, slow breaths before raising his head to meet Taegan's eyes once more.

"No, I'm glad you're here," he replied, and Taegan stifled a slight grin at that. "I was worried your presence might be the spark that finally lit the flame of whatever was brewing, but it seems it was on the way, regardless of whether you were here. So I'm glad you stayed." He grimaced, and a dark sort of amusement trickled from the bond. "It seems like you're finally going to get the battle against the orcs you've always wanted."

Taegan could not stop himself from laughing aloud at that, though it was a dry and humorless laugh.

"I suppose so," he said, nodding. "Though I have to say it's not nearly as exciting a prospect as I had once hoped."

"Listen," Zorvut said, his tone suddenly much more serious. He pulled away from their embrace enough to look Taegan directly in the eye, his grip tightening around Taegan's arms to hold him firmly in place. "I know how strong a fighter you are, how capable a leader you are. I trust you completely. Do you understand?"

Taegan blinked, taken aback at his sudden sternness. "Yes, I understand."

"I trust you completely," Zorvut repeated, then sighed. "But I don't know anything about what Zesh is planning. And it's entirely likely that he'll challenge me to single combat, the way I did with Hrul. In fact, I would be surprised if he doesn't. If it comes to that... I'm still injured, and I won't have the surprise of my magic against him. So if things take a turn for the worse... Taegan, if it seems like it's going to be a losing battle, I want you to take as many elves as you can rally and go home. Back to Aefraya."

Taegan frowned, Zorvut's words not processing right away. Go home? Why would he ever do that?

"What?" he asked, shaking his head. "I won't leave you, Zorvut."

"I'm serious," Zorvut said, releasing Taegan for just a brief moment to instead grasp his hands, meeting his eyes without wavering. "You can't—you can't die here, Taegan. Your father needs you. Your people need you. You have so, so much longer to live."

His voice broke at that, and for the first time a burst of grief escaped the bond, instantly bringing tears to Taegan's eyes as well. "You have so many years ahead of you, Taegan. I don't want to be the cause of your wasted potential. If things get bad, please, *please* just go. I want you to live, to go home, so you can regroup and find another way to end the war. My place is here, and if I die, I die. But you... You can still do so much more. You can go on to be happy and become king and have lots of—lots of little princes and princesses running around."

Taegan was shaking his head rapidly without even realizing it. "My place is here, too, with you," he protested, his voice suddenly hoarse.

"I need you to promise me," Zorvut insisted, squeezing his hands. His grip trembled, but his gaze was unwavering. "I beg of you. Please, please just promise me, if it seems hopeless, you'll protect yourself first and go home to Aefraya."

He wanted to protest, to scream, to insist that he could not possibly go on without Zorvut. The thought of running away and leaving Zorvut to die made him sick to even consider, but the flood of despair and fear coming from the bond was more than he could withstand, drowning out every word before he could even formulate a sentence. Zorvut had kept a tight grip on his emotions since reuniting, but the strength of his conviction proved too much to hold back now.

"I promise," Taegan whispered, looking down at where his hands were clasping Zorvut's, gripping him tightly to keep them from trembling, though the effort was in vain. He did not want to, but he could not bring himself to say anything else. "I promise."

The words hung heavy between them for a long moment, silence settling over them until finally Zorvut released Taegan's hands to wipe his own eyes, glancing away.

"Thank you," he said, his voice gravelly with emotion. "I... That means a lot to me, Taegan. I don't want things to turn out that way, but if they do, knowing you'll be okay will be a small comfort."

He did not know what to say. It was understandable, but the thought of fleeing while Zorvut stayed to die was of no comfort to him at all. His feelings must have been clear through the bond as Zorvut reached out to softly touch his arm once again.

"I know it's a lot to ask," he said. "I know. But this shouldn't be your hill to die on."

"But it should be yours?" Taegan asked, unable to bite back the words. "Zorvut, not even a month ago, half of these people would have marched on Aefraya without a second thought. They didn't hesitate to take up arms again when Hrul called off the treaty. It's not your hill to die on, either!"

"It is," Zorvut insisted, his brows furrowing. "It is, Taegan. When I killed Hrul and took his title, it became my place, for better or for worse."

He bit his lip, looking away. How could he argue with that?

"You're too noble for your own good," he spat, and Zorvut laughed weakly, shaking his head.

"I'm sorry," he said softly, and Taegan leaned against him again. Despite his tumultuous emotions, there was still comfort in his embrace. "I'm going to do everything I can to make sure it doesn't come to that. And I know you will, too."

The next day showed no sign of an invading army, but in the afternoon, Gorza came to them again with more information. One of their scouts had spotted Zesh and his group late the evening before and rode hard through the night to return with the news.

"The good news is that the scout thinks Zesh has fifty or fewer warriors with him, which is manageable even if they're all on horseback," she said, Zorvut looking pensively down at his hands clasped tightly together on the table in front of him as he listened. "The bad news is that he will definitely be here tomorrow. We should make whatever preparations we can now to be ready."

The rest of the day was a whirlwind of making sure every capable warrior that remained in Drol Kuggradh was briefed and prepared for battle. Luckily for Taegan, with as many elves as there were still in the city, they outfitted him with decent armor and weapons without too much issue. It was not his own personal bow, but it was military-grade and perfectly serviceable.

Sleep was a struggle that night. For all the worry Taegan tried to push from his mind, every time he started to feel a little more calm and a little less anxious, he would only feel Zorvut's worry more acutely. It was like a cold, aching muscle in the back of his head that he couldn't unclench, and when he looked back over at Zorvut in bed next to him, he could see the half-orc's eyes open and staring up at the ceiling.

After a long while of fruitlessly trying to sleep, he pushed himself up into a sitting position, and Zorvut's eyes flicked over to look at him.

"I can't sleep," he said softly, and without waiting for a response, he swung his leg over Zorvut's waist and straddled him, pushing his hands under his shirt.

"Taegan," Zorvut said softly, brows furrowed, barely discernible in the darkness.

"If this is our last night together," Taegan said, rocking his hips slowly. "Then I want to spend it making love to my husband."

For a moment Zorvut did not respond, and in the silence Taegan felt suddenly doubtful. He nearly moved to get off of Zorvut when finally the familiar echo of arousal came through the bond, and Zorvut propped himself up on his elbows to look more closely at him.

"Okay," he said quietly, nodding, and Taegan stifled a self-satisfied grin. He could feel Zorvut becoming hard underneath him, and he pulled away just enough to pull down his underwear as Zorvut pulled off his shirt.

He made a soft, startled noise as Zorvut's rough hands pushed under his own shirt, yanking it off in one swift movement—but it quickly became a moan as the half-orc ran his hands down the length of his torso, brushing over his nipples and feeling along each divot between his abs.

"Come here," Zorvut said, his voice gravelly, and he pulled Taegan down so he was laying with their chests pressed together, skin-to-skin along the length of their torsos. Taegan pressed his face into Zorvut's shoulder, and for a moment the only sound was the soft slide of Zorvut's hands idly running up and down his back and his fingers running through his hair. Despite how eagerly hard his cock was, he was loath to be the first to break away from the intimate moment, so he closed his eyes and let himself revel in the soft pleasure of Zorvut's fingers on his skin.

"I love you," he breathed, and peppered soft kisses along Zorvut's neck and collarbones. "I love you so much."

"I love you too," Zorvut murmured, his voice a deep rumble in Taegan's ear pressed against his chest.

The desire resounding through the bond was too much for Taegan to hold back anymore, so he pushed himself back up to straddle Zorvut, letting out a soft moan at the hard head of his cock that pressed against him as he settled his weight onto Zorvut's hips. When he looked down at Zorvut's face, the half-orc's eyes were trained on his cock, watching hungrily as they moved against each other.

"Look at me," he said, and Zorvut glanced up to meet his gaze. Their eyes locked on each other's, Taegan reached back and pressed the head of Zorvut's cock against his entrance already soaked with slick and lowered himself onto it. Arousal burst white-hot through the bond as they both gasped and Taegan sank down to bury Zorvut to the hilt inside him.

"Gods, Taegan," Zorvut groaned, his head falling back against their pillows. "You feel so good."

"Show me," Taegan begged, squeezing his eyes shut at the sudden overwhelming fullness deep within him. His mouth fell open with a cry of pleasure as Zorvut moved inside him, sending his vision alight with stars as his body was opened up. It was a slow, decadent movement, relishing in every tiny touch of friction, not at all the frantic and needy coupling they had indulged in after having spent so long apart. Taegan could feel the heat of Zorvut's gaze on him, watching the space where their bodies joined with an unwavering intensity—he could feel the concentration through the bond underneath the physical sensation flooding through it, as if he were committing the moment to memory as much as he possibly could.

Zorvut's hands had settled on his hips for a moment, but after a few long, slow thrusts his hands wandered again, running smoothly down his thighs only to trail back up his torso, rubbing hard against his nipples that elicited a gasp of surprise. Then one hand lowered to touch his cock, the other still tweaking one nipple, and Taegan moaned at the sudden overstimulation. His whole body felt alight with radiating heat, and even though Zorvut moved so slowly inside him, he could already tell he was close.

"I'm—I'm—" he panted, but his words dissolved into a shuddering gasp as he came.

"See how good you feel?" Zorvut growled, his voice thick with heat as he squeezed and milked every drop of come out of him.

"How good you make me feel," Taegan replied when he could speak again, panting for breath. Zorvut shifted under him, and suddenly he was lying on the bed with the half-orc on top of him. Instinctively, Taegan wrapped his legs around Zorvut's waist, his hands coming up to his shoulders and trailing along his back, feeling the hard muscle and raised skin where his body was scarred from past battles and wounds.

"You're so beautiful," Zorvut murmured, his eyes running up and down Taegan's body. He paused for a moment to look at him, and Taegan glanced away, feeling suddenly shy under the intensity of his gaze. "You are. I've been so lucky. I'm so lucky you're mine." His hips moved again, thrusting into Taegan faster now.

"I'm yours," Taegan agreed, nodding his head. Pleasure cascaded through the bond as if it were his own cock being squeezed and stroked again. He could hardly catch his breath for how intense every sensation felt, how every nerve in his body tingled with heat, with energy. One of Zorvut's hands grabbed his hip, bracing him against his body as his pace quickened, fucking him hard and fast.

"Fuck," Zorvut groaned against Taegan's shoulder, and he could feel how close he was. Taegan clenched around Zorvut's cock and they both cried aloud at the sensation, Zorvut giving only a few more hard thrusts before he was coming. Taegan moaned faintly as he could feel himself being filled with hot, thick liquid as Zorvut panted and gasped against his neck. "Gods, I wish I could fuck you forever."

For one brief instant Taegan wished desperately he was in heat, that when Zorvut had filled him with his seed, he could carry a piece of him forever, no matter how things turned out—and his thought must have been clear through the bond as Zorvut suddenly burst into a ragged sob, pressing his face into Taegan's shoulder.

"I want that too," he murmured, and his tremulous voice was the closest to a frightened whimper Taegan had ever heard from him. He squeezed his eyes shut against his own tears as his arms tightened around Zorvut's shoulders, pulling him closer. "I want to stay with you, I want to have children with you. I don't want to die. I don't—Taegan, I don't want to die."

"You won't die," Taegan replied, his voice breaking. "You won't. I won't let you. You're going to win, just like you did before, and we're going to unite our kingdoms and you're going to grow old and see your children and grandchildren grow up, too. I promise. I promise."

He could feel Zorvut tremble in his arms, tears dripping from the half-orc's face and wetting the skin of his neck and shoulders. Had he ever been so vulnerable before? The absolute anguish pouring from the bond was like a flayed nerve against the cold air, and he squeezed his eyes shut against his own tears that burned against his eyelids. He wouldn't let Zorvut die. He couldn't. He may have promised Zorvut he would protect himself, but it wouldn't stop him from doing everything he could to protect Zorvut first.

"I'm sorry," Zorvut breathed after a long moment, pushing himself up to look down at Taegan. Even in the dark, he could see the half-orc's eyes were puffy and his face flushed. "I didn't mean to... to have things end like that."

"Don't apologize," Taegan replied quickly, cupping Zorvut's face in one hand. "You're my husband. Don't ever apologize to me for your emotions."

"My husband," Zorvut repeated softly, his eyelids closing as he pressed his face into Taegan's hand. "My husband."

They remained in tender silence for a long moment, both unmoving and unwilling to break the contact, until finally Zorvut took in a long, shuddering breath and pulled Taegan to the edge of the bed. Slowly he eased his softened cock out of Taegan's body—Taegan let out a sharp hiss as they separated and a stream of still-warm come and slick spilled out of him.

When they had cleaned up, Zorvut took Taegan into his arms again and carried him back to bed, despite the elf's playful protests.

"I want to hold you," he murmured as they settled into bed, cradling Taegan against his chest. "Even if I don't sleep. I want to hold you all night."

Taegan hesitated, then nodded. He shifted until he was comfortable, laying atop Zorvut's torso with his face pressed into the crook of his shoulder, Zorvut's arms draped loosely around his waist.

"I love you," he whispered as he closed his eyes, and it repeated in his head with every slow, even breath he took until he fell asleep. *I love you. I love you. I love you.*

CHAPTER FIFTEEN
TAEGAN

Taegan was quite sure neither he nor Zorvut truly slept, at least not long enough to matter. He dozed on and off through the night, but each time he opened his eyes or shifted against Zorvut, the half-orc's golden eyes were gleaming down at him and he could feel a hard knot of anxiety in the back of his head. Eventually the sun was coming up through the window when he opened his eyes again, which was when Zorvut finally moved, gently releasing him from his arms and shifting him onto the blankets before getting up with a sigh. Taegan tried to sleep a bit longer, but it was a futile effort, and before long he too stumbled out of bed.

Zorvut was downstairs in their small kitchen, blankly looking out the window with a steaming mug of coffee in his hands. He gave a slight start at the sound of Taegan coming down the stone stairs. His eyes were bleary and sunken when he glanced over at Taegan—if he had any doubt before, now he was certain the poor man hadn't slept at all. For an instant he wondered, sadly, if he had been so afraid the morning he was set to arrive in Drol Kuggradh to face Hrul, just over a week ago.

"Coffee?" Zorvut offered, his voice hoarse. He cleared his throat, offering the mug toward Taegan, who shook his head.

"No, thank you," he replied softly, and came to stand next to him. They stood, silent and observant, at the window to watch as the first rays of morning light spread over the city. It was quiet, and the sunrise was beautiful. Despite everything, the knot of nerves in the back of his head relaxed gradually into a soft contentment.

But, eventually, the peaceful moment came to an end. They dressed—Taegan wavered between his normal clothes and his armor for a long while, eventually donning the armor after helping Zorvut put on a breastplate. He slung his bow and quiver across his back and followed the half-orc out of the tower and into the misty morning.

Despite their nerves and the anxious quiet that seemed to permeate the city and all its residents, the first few hours of the day were uneventful. But that was almost worse, Taegan thought—it only made the morning feel longer, the uncertainty more excruciating.

A bit before midday, though, Gorza came to find them again. She burst through the flaps of the tent speaking breathlessly in orcish, but hesitated and switched to elvish when she saw Taegan and the elven soldiers they were sitting with.

"They've been spotted again," she said, panting as she glanced between them and the small group of orcish warriors that were also present. "It'll only be another hour or two now."

"We'll meet them in the field," Zorvut said quickly—they had been discussing the plan of attack, and everyone seemed to agree that fighting in the city would be a disadvantage to be avoided if at all possible. "I'll meet with your scout first. Taegan, make sure the message is passed along to every elven warrior in the city. I want every fighter stationed along the western wall." Taegan nodded, as did the elves sitting with them, but already Zorvut had turned his attention to the handful of orcs waiting for his command, barking out a gruff order before the group of them dispersed with a nod of acknowledgment.

Surprisingly, there was very little anxiety coming from the bond now, and Zorvut seemed cool and collected as he gave commands—a stark contrast to his vulnerability the night before, but Taegan supposed that was to be expected. He was a warrior, a warlord now, and so it was only fitting that he would keep his emotions under tight control. Still, it gave him pause.

He left with the elven soldiers to pass the information on to Captain Kyrenic, and did not see Zorvut again until he was atop his horse and riding for the western gate. It was strange, finally going into battle against the orcs the way he thought he would for so much of his life, knowing he was now fighting alongside them, too.

Zorvut was a vision atop his own warhorse, Taegan's breath catching in his chest when he came into view—Graksh't was always an intimidating sight, as such a massive beast, but the armor adorning him made him all the more fearsome. And Zorvut was covered with war paint, not unlike the paint he'd worn on their wedding day, though this time it was much more aggressive, somehow. A vivid crimson, it curled up from his eyes like flames and accentuated every muscle of his bare arms. He had never seen Zorvut looking so fierce, but it was strangely fitting, and atop Graksh't he did not look all that much shorter than any of the orcs surrounding him also in armor and war paint, and no less intimidating.

From the bond he could feel a grim determination more than anything else, but as he drew closer and Zorvut caught sight of him, relief overpowered it.

"I'm here," Taegan said, pulling up alongside him. It seemed every time they were on horseback together Taegan had a different horse—this one was a black gelding that had been given to him as a gift from a merchant Zorvut had been meeting with that was too small for an adult orc to ride, but still taller than any horse he'd rode before. "We're all ready. Everyone's in position."

"Good," Zorvut said with a nod, then leaned over to squeeze Taegan's shoulder. "I'm glad to see you. You look... I don't know. It suits you somehow. Being up here in your armor."

Taegan grinned up at him. "Strange, I was just thinking the same of you. Who painted you? It looks truly fearsome."

Zorvut laughed at that. "Myself, mainly, though Gorza helped me. Mostly symbols of luck and victory, though this—" He pointed at his eyes. "—was her idea."

"Where is Gorza?" he asked, glancing around. He did not see her; he did not recognize any of the orcs leading the charge, but they were equally vicious in appearance with their own paint and armored horses.

"Watching from the wall," Zorvut replied, looking decidedly less amused now. "I asked her to stay back and watch with the guard, so she can give the order to try to evacuate as many as possible if Zesh's group is able to break through, or... Or if there's a splinter group in the city waiting on his command to come from behind."

Taegan frowned at that. "You think there might be that many?"

"No, probably not. I think whatever group here in the city that might be loyal to Zesh and has any knowledge of this would be quite small, but if they take us by surprise, they don't need many."

"Wise of you," Taegan replied, though he shot an anxious glance over at the wall. That could certainly be a problem.

"Now we wait," Zorvut sighed, his gaze out on the horizon. With the craggy hills surrounding Drol Kuggradh, visibility did not extend very far from the city. "Once the horn sounds from the tower, we'll start marching west. I would expect he knows, or at least suspects, that we know he's coming, so I think he'll just be coming up the main road."

Taegan nodded, following his gaze. The road was not particularly wide, especially for those on horseback, and the land became more rocky and hilly the further west it extended. There would be room for a battle, certainly, but close combat could end up being quite close. He would have to stay as far away as possible—the last thing he wanted was to be in close combat with an orc twice his size. And Zorvut had explained to him that if Zesh did challenge him to single combat—which he expected would happen—Taegan and the elves mustn't interfere, no matter how dire the situation became. These challenges were revered, almost sacred, and any interlopers were to be slain.

Taegan hated it, but had agreed not to interfere, so he would remain with the rest of the elves.But this was it; the charge he had dreamed of leading since he was old enough to swing a sword. For all the fear that still burned like bile in his chest, he also had a strange sense of mounting excitement. The prospect of seeing their common enemy, drawing his bow as he shouted commands to the elves behind him... Finally, it seemed, some of his lifelong training would pay off.

Zorvut glanced over at him wordlessly, feeling his anticipation, and a faint amusement flickered from the bond but otherwise his expression was unreadable.

He was not sure how much longer they waited, everyone glancing between each other nervously but no one speaking. It felt like a long while, but each time he glanced up at the sky it seemed the sun hadn't changed positions at all, so although it felt like hours, he doubted it was more than perhaps thirty minutes.

And then, finally—the signal that they had all been waiting silently for. A long blare of the warning horn from the wall shattered through the nervous silence, reverberating through Taegan's ribs as his heart started to pound. This was truly it.

Next to him Zorvut shouted something in orcish, drawing his sword. A resounding, guttural shout answered him from the orcs behind them.

"We march!" Taegan exclaimed, echoed by Captain Kyrenic far behind him, and he pressed his heels into the horse's sides, and they were off.

He did not see them yet, and the sound of hooves on dirt and stone were almost certainly from their own group, but he thought he could just make out the noise of more horses from a distance. He glanced over at Zorvut, but the half-orc's gaze was firmly ahead of him, his brows furrowed and his lips pulled taut in a grim frown around his tusks.

The rebel orcs did not come into view until they crested a low hill, and finally Taegan could see them—all on horseback, but even at first glance, decidedly fewer than the group they led. They were around three hundred feet away, maybe a bit further, but just as the first scout had reported, he could see only fifty, maybe sixty at most. Compared to the nearly fifty elves behind him, and easily twice as many orcs, Zesh and his group were entirely outnumbered. A strange relief flooded him at the same time as a spike of adrenaline at the sight, and he wasn't sure which of the feelings was his and which was Zorvut's.

A second horn sounded, this one from ahead of them. They had been spotted, too.

Zorvut glanced at him and nodded. From here, the elves and other archers would have a solid vantage point and would be harder to reach. Taegan nodded in return, already pulling an arrow from his quiver.

"Don't wait. No mercy," Zorvut barked in gruff elvish, before turning away and shouting out a command in orcish. His voice was deep and harsh as he roared, and was quickly echoed by other orcs responding to his call. Graksh't broke into a gallop as the melee warriors plunged ahead.

"Archers to me!" Taegan exclaimed, and though he did not turn to look, he could hear the sound of many more horses approaching and scattering behind him. This far away, he could not tell which orc was Zesh, so he picked out the biggest of the group and aimed his arrow. "And fire!"

His arrow was the first to soar high over the heads of the orcs that had galloped down the hill, but it was soon joined by many others. He watched it arc through the air and sink deep into the shoulder of the figure he had aimed for—he could see the orc jerk back in pain, his mouth open in a shout, but lost sight of him in the chaos as many more arrows rained down over the group.

The sounds of fighting erupted from the bottom of the hill as Zorvut and his warriors met the invading orcs, the clashing of swords ringing out over shouts and screams. Where was Zorvut? Already it was harder to tell which were allies and which were enemies—and then there was a flash of light, a flaming sword to find him by.

"Don't lose sight of our allies!" he called out. "Zorvut bears the flaming sword! Whoever he attacks is an enemy!"

All he could feel from the bond was a steady flood of adrenaline, drowning out everything else. Or maybe it was his own? It was hard to tell, impossible to separate their feelings when they were both in such a heightened state. His heart was hammering in his chest, of that he was certain. But the exhilaration flooding him now had very little fear; in the rush of the moment, it almost seemed silly that he had ever been afraid. If they were careful, if they played it smart, surely they would easily be victorious.

There was a second horn call then, from behind them, but it cut off abruptly. With a frown, Taegan looked back, just in time to see a guard tumbling from the wall to the earth below. He winced at the sight, and glancing up at the top of the wall, he could see another orc had shoved the guard. Panic spiked in him as he thought it might be Gorza, but then he saw her further along on the wall, drawing her weapon and pointing not at the assailant but down at the ground beneath them.

From the path behind them, a band of orcs were riding out on horseback, weapons drawn, heading right for them.

"We're being attacked from behind," he called out, and he could hear the captain shouting something out next to him, but already he was acting on instinct, drawing an arrow. The group that charged them was small, no more than ten—if they could take them out quickly, before they even could reach the elves, they would pose no threat to Zorvut or the others. It looked like only the one was up on the wall, turning away from Gorza and the other guards to presumably flee and join the charge. He was far away and the angle would be tricky, but Taegan was a good shot. He took in a long, steadying breath, and released the bowstring.

His arrow found the throat of the orc on the wall, and his whole body jerked in pained shock, reaching instinctively for the arrow before collapsing out of sight. One problem taken care of, at least.

Taegan drew another, but a volley was already following, raining down on the newcomers. They were closer, easier to spot, and the shower of arrows struck true. Several of the orcs were hit, some falling to the ground and some clinging, wounded, to their mounts—and some horses cried out in fear and pain as they were caught up in the volley, too. The few that remained uninjured—now only three, each with arrows sticking out of their shields—slowed and hesitated.

No mercy, Taegan remembered, Zorvut's words echoing in his head. Gritting his teeth, he drew another arrow.

"Take all of them out!" he commanded, and released the arrow. It whistled through the air and sunk deep into the chest of one of the three orcs; the figure froze, his horse still running forward, but the reins slipped from his hands as he reached up to grasp the bolt uselessly and tumbled out of the saddle. He watched as more arrows struck the remaining two and their lifeless bodies slumped over their horses that dashed away in fear.

Taegan's eyes lingered on the bodies of the orcs for a moment, then he looked back toward the wall, toward the guard who had sounded the alarm before being pushed off. If the guard had not made the horn call, cut off as it was, that could have gone much differently. He wasn't sure what exactly the orc custom might be for a burial with honors, but he made a mental note to ask later, if they made it.

If they made it. That shook him from his thoughts, and he turned away from the wall to look down to where Zorvut and the others were fighting.

The other elves had wasted no time in turning their attention back to the fight as another volley of arrows soared down from atop the hill, showering the skirmish with deadly bolts once again. A few orcs fell, but as he scanned the battleground he was growing less and less sure of which were his allies and which were enemy orcs.

"Let's draw closer," he said to Captain Kyrenic next to him; the other elf nodded in agreement, though his eyes remained trained on the battlefield. "Archers, stay with me!" he shouted out, and with a nudge of his heels, his gelding trotted down the hill. He didn't want to get too near to the fighting, so he moved at a cautious pace, pulling back on the reins the moment they seemed right on the cusp of being too close.

From his new vantage point, it was easier to see the battle; still he could not make out exactly where Zesh was, but it seemed his force had been pushed back considerably. Zorvut was easy to pick out with his flaming sword—and although it made him a target for the enemy orcs as well, he seemed to be holding his own. Even from a distance, Taegan could tell the orcs around him were trying to protect him. A few dead orcs and horses were already on the ground, and none of them were immediately recognizable to Taegan. So far, everything was going about as well as he could hope for, and he drew another arrow.

"Zorvut!"

A roar broke through the noise of battle, drawing every eye—and the moment Taegan saw the new orc approaching at a gallop on his own horse, he knew it was Zesh. The massive figure held a huge battle axe in his hand much like the one Hrul had carried, a furious snarl on his face that was painted with blood-red symbols that extended all the way around his shaved skull and down his neck to disappear under the armor he wore. Ten more orcs followed him, all of them painted as well. Zesh shouted out something in orcish that Taegan did not understand, but the activity on the battlefield seemed to pause, everyone hesitating and watching as the force approached. A hot tendril of fear came through the bond, quickly followed by that familiar grim determination he had felt from Zorvut so often in the past day.

"He's challenged Zorvut to single combat," Taegan said softly, understanding dawning on him. "They know they're outnumbered. It's the only way he'd be able to win."

He hesitated, wanting to draw closer, but he could see Zorvut look back toward him from below. Their eyes met, and from the bond he could hear clearly—- Remember. Promise.

Guilt ached in his chest and, for a moment, so did fear, sparking anew. But he bit his lip and nodded once, sharply, and after a moment Zorvut nodded in response and turned away to face Zesh. They had slowed to a careful walk, and the crowd parted around them as Zesh leapt from his horse and took a few steps toward Zorvut.

The flames of his sword flickered and died, and with an answer that Taegan could not quite make out, he too dismounted from Graksh't. The orc that had been behind Zorvut took the reins and pulled the stallion away, and the entire group spread out to create a loose circle around the two brothers.

Half-brothers, Taegan reminded himself, though that did not make the situation feel any less bleak to him. Though he had no siblings of his own, it still seemed a terrible prospect to have to face a brother in battle. The sentiment seemed mirrored in the bond—clearly Zorvut did not want to fight him either, but more than that he did not want Drol Kuggradh to come under Zesh's rule, and he did not want the peace treaty to be struck down yet again.

"Captain," Taegan said, barely above a whisper, as they watched the orcs circle each other, speaking to each other in voices too low to carry up the hill. "If things go poorly, if... If Zorvut should fall, I want you to give the command for all elves to retreat."

He could practically feel Kyrenic hesitating next to him, but he could not tear his eyes away from Zorvut.

"Yes, my prince," the strained reply finally came, and Taegan nodded. The thought made him feel just as wretched, but he had given Zorvut his word.

From below, the tension broke as a shout erupted from the crowd and Zesh lunged, his great axe whistling through the air.

Chapter Sixteen
Zorvut

Zorvut did his best to push every thought from his head as Zesh lunged at him, acting on instinct as he leapt backward away from the axe screaming through the air toward him. Zesh was strong and bulky even by orc standards, and he relied on that to win. If he could just keep dodging and outsmarting him, he could keep the upper hand.

The blade of the massive axe plowed into the hard earth in front of him as Zesh missed, snarling up at him as he wrenched it free.

"You're a fucking traitor," Zesh growled, lifting the weapon above his head again. "You killed my father, you bastard!"

He couldn't let Zesh's words distract him, much as they stung. Zorvut grit his teeth, pulling threads of fire to his sword, and charged at Zesh before he could bring his axe down as his own blade erupted back into flame.

The element of surprise that had given him the upper hand against Hrul was gone now, but it was still a tool that he had that Zesh did not. Even though he was expecting the fiery sword, it extended Zorvut's reach and made Zesh more cautious about getting too close to him. And he had the lightning javelin—though that was slower to summon, if he could get some decent distance between them, that might be a weapon Zesh couldn't foresee.

Zesh's axe knocked away his blade, but he used the momentum to swing it in a wide arc and bring it back up. It scraped against Zesh's metal armor with a terrible screeching sound, and the orc let out a hiss of pain as a line of red heat smoldered in its path for an instant before fading and cooling.

"Dammit," Zesh hissed, wincing as he took a stumbling step away. Zorvut swung again, taking advantage of his brief distraction. He aimed for the hand that was holding the greataxe, catching him in the wrist. Zesh howled as he stumbled backward; he kept his grip on the axe, but blood was pouring from his hand.

Zorvut took a few quick steps back, putting more distance between them as Zesh struggled with his wounded wrist. He couldn't let up, not for a second—he drew back his free hand as if about to throw a spear, twisting threads of fire into lightning in his hand. Zesh's head snapped up to look at him as thunder began to crackle audibly, but it was already too late as he hurled the handful of lightning at his brother. It flashed through the air for a brief instant before crashing into his chest, sending the orc falling back with a resounding thud. The wind had clearly been knocked out of him as he gasped and quivered on the floor.

A faint tendril of hope rose up in him, but he didn't let himself feel it for too long, pushing it away before it might reach Taegan. It wasn't over until it was over.

He took a few slow steps toward Zesh as he lay groaning on the ground, and as he stood over him with his sword pointing at his chest, he growled, "Yield."

Zesh's eyes snapped open to glare at him.

"Fuck you," he spat, and before Zorvut could react, the orc swung up one of his legs and kicked him squarely in the groin. Pain exploded through him as he stumbled away, biting back a cry—even from the distance between them he heard Taegan yelp as the terrible sensation must have burst through the bond to him as well. The sickening pain radiating all the way up his belly into his throat made him gag, but he could hear Zesh trying to stand up. Zorvut pulled the pain away from the bond in the back of his head as much as he could and staggered to his feet. Across from him Zesh had stood too, but he was struggling to lift his axe with the deep gash in his wrist gushing blood onto the handle. With a muttered curse, Zesh grabbed the weapon with his other hand, lifting it with a wobbling grip.

Zesh was still quick even though his aim was worse, and he charged Zorvut before he could catch his breath. He lifted his sword to parry but Zesh was already too close, and the axe came down on his shoulder and pushed him back to the ground. With his weakened grip in his non-dominant hand, it was painful and would certainly leave a terrible bruise, but it didn't feel as if anything was broken or bleeding as he rolled away and struggled to get onto his feet. He had to ignore it. He had to keep fighting.

But Zesh had not let up at all and was already lifting his axe for another swing while Zorvut was still crouched on the ground—he raised his sword to protect himself instinctually, but the flames left in its path remained in place, creating a column of fire between him and Zesh. It blocked his vision, but he could hear Zesh stumble back in shock. If it had not come from his own sword, Zorvut might have leapt away in surprise too, unsure of how he had created a shield of flame—not that he could complain about it. If Zesh had landed another hit while he was already down...

He couldn't let himself think about that. Zorvut scrambled to his feet as the flames dissipated, before Zesh could take advantage of his surprise. The flames around his sword had flickered out when the shield of flame died, and he re-ignited them with a growl. He could feel the exhaustion creeping into the edges of his thoughts—a solid lightning bolt or a flurry of ice could be enough to incapacitate Zesh more effectively, but the fire shield seemed to have taken more out of him than just igniting the sword, and he doubted he had the energy to summon something of that magnitude.

Zesh was still maintaining a cautious distance from him, and they circled each other for a moment, neither moving as quickly as they had been moments before. Every step sent pain radiating anew up into his stomach and down his legs, but he forced himself to keep walking and raised his sword once more.

"Come on, then," he goaded, but Zesh only glared at him, holding his axe at the ready. Neither moved for a moment, so Zorvut lunged at him with a heavy swing of his sword.

Embers scattered to the ground as Zesh blocked with his axe, though it wavered in his non-dominant hand. They slashed at each other, parrying and blocking and dodging, each trying to be the one to land a solid blow first. But neither could get a hit on the other, and after a shower of embers sprayed back nearly into his face, Zorvut leapt away before Zesh could try to strike him again.

"Come on!" the orc growled at him, baring his tusks with a frenzied snarl. "Coward!"

Zorvut bit his lip, breathing hard. As it was, they were essentially at a stalemate. Even with his flaming sword and Zesh at a disadvantage with his wounded wrist, the orc was just that much bigger than him—and he did not want the battle to last long enough to see whose endurance would win out. He had to end things.

Fight! The thought came through the bond as clearly as if Taegan was shouting it, though he wouldn't risk looking up toward the hill to look for him. You have to fight!

He grabbed onto the thought instinctually, holding the words, Taegan's voice, in his mind—and, somehow, pulled threads of fire from the magic of their bond, twisting them into lightning in his hands. He had no idea how he'd done it, but he did. For all the magic he had been taught there was so much more he didn't understand. He stepped back, pulled his arm back in the same throwing motion—

Zesh recognized the move now, and a hateful glare crossed his face as he seemed to weigh his options, hesitating for the split second it took for the lighting bolt to crackle to life before lunging at Zorvut again. But the lightning was already leaving Zorvut's fingertips, though he was too close now; it exploded with a thunderclap into Zesh's chest, but the force of it knocked Zorvut backward, too.

For an instant, he was blind, and all he could feel was the pounding in his head, a ringing in his ears. Every one of his muscles pulsed with pain, and for a moment he doubted he had the strength to stand again.

Get up! He could hear Taegan's voice in his head just barely breaking through, though his vision was still swimming. *Please get up!*

With a groan, he pushed himself back up to his feet, blinking a few times until his blurry vision crept back into focus. Every inch of his body felt weighed down with lead, slow and agonizing to move. Zesh had fallen no more than twenty feet from him, his metal breastplate steaming with heat from the thunderbolt.

"Yield," Zorvut said again, a ragged gasp as he stumbled toward his brother. "Just yield."

But Zesh would not yield—he could see it in his eyes through the dazed, wounded expression on his face. There was no mistaking the rage, the fury, behind those eyes even before his face twisted into a snarl when he caught sight of Zorvut, shaking his head in proud refusal.

He had to end it. Zorvut kicked the axe away before Zesh could tighten his grip and stood over the orc. He drew in every last ounce of energy he had left, reaching for the spot in the back of his head where the bond sat to pull everything he could from it, and formed a whirling globe of ice and snow between his hands. Letting out a wordless roar of exertion, he pushed it down, aiming not for Zesh's chest but his arm, the one he had slashed at the wrist.

Zesh shouted in startled pain as ice splintered up the limb, leaving it heavy and frozen to the ground. He was stuck, and he realized it as he struggled to stand or roll or do anything to get further away from Zorvut—but could not.

"Do you yield?" Zorvut asked again, pressing his boot to Zesh's chest. This time, the words sounded like a plea even to his own ears.

"Never," Zesh growled, writhing under his foot. "Never!"

Zorvut took in a slow breath. This felt a hundred times worse than killing Hrul, but he had no choice. The weight of every orc in Drol Kuggradh was on his shoulders now.

He raised his sword over his head and brought it crashing down to Zesh's arm with a shout. The sound of the blade slicing through bone and piercing the earth beneath was not the sound of tearing flesh, but the shattering of ice—and with a shriek of agony, Zesh's arm was not cut from his body but broken off of it like glass, the forearm left whole but everything below the shoulder joint breaking apart in jagged pieces. Though there was no blood, the frozen chunks of flesh were somehow worse, and Zorvut looked away from the shattered limb to Zesh's horrified face.

"My arm!" he screamed when he could finally form words, his features twisted in pain and shock. "You cut off my fucking arm!"

"I don't want to kill you," Zorvut growled, keeping his weight on Zesh's chest so he couldn't crawl away. "Yield. Just yield!"

Tears streamed down Zesh's face as he glared up at Zorvut, but the facade lasted only a moment.

"I yield," he wailed, his head falling back to hit the ground. "You bastard! You fucking traitor, I yield!"

Zorvut pulled his foot off the other orc's chest, taking in a long, slow breath as he looked down at him.

"It's over," he called out, looking up for the first time at the orcs that surrounded them in a circle. "Get him a healer."

There was a beat of silence as he looked over the stunned expressions of the orcs who had come with Zesh, the cautiously optimistic looks of those who had accompanied him—and then he looked up the hill for Taegan.

His husband was still atop his horse, perched cautiously in the same spot with the other elves surrounding him, but even from this distance, he could see his eyes welling with tears. He had been so focused that he hadn't felt the flood of relief coming from the bond, though he did not need to feel it to see it plain as day on Taegan's face.

He managed a slight smile and a nod, but now that he was not running on pure adrenaline, his body ached with fatigue, his wounds catching up with him. He turned back to watch two orcs uncertainly helping Zesh to his feet, and one of his warriors came up to him with an eager grin. The orc said something, but it sounded distant and muffled.

Zorvut frowned. "What?"

How had it gotten so dark? It was still barely midday, he thought, and the slightly overcast sky didn't seem like it would rain, yet everything was rapidly becoming dim. He felt dizzy, the ground rolling beneath his feet.

The orc spoke to him once more, but still he couldn't understand—he shook his head, and looked toward Taegan again, but his vision was going blurry, and dark, and suddenly the air around him felt as cold as ice. He looked for Taegan, but everything had gone pitch black.

Chapter Seventeen
Taegan

"No news, then?"

Taegan glanced up at Gorza, sitting across from him in their parlor. Just a moment ago, she had been updating him on the new trade routes being proposed by the merchant's association, but the conversation had lapsed into uncertain silence. From the look on her face, he did not need to guess what she was referring to.

"Nothing different from yesterday," Taegan replied with a sigh, leaning back. "It's just as I told you. The healers don't think his life is in any danger now, but his body is still recovering. That between the magic and his injuries, there was no energy left, or—something like that. They say he'll wake up once he's ready, but..." He shrugged, pressing his lips together. "I don't know. I'm trying not to worry about it yet. They don't seem concerned, so... And it's only been a few days. I'll wait to worry until it's been closer to a few weeks."

"Well, it's been a week now," Gorza said in a teasing tone, a slight smile spreading across her face. Taegan grimaced at that.

"Gods, has it really?" he groaned. "The days are all just running together, I suppose." They both chuckled nervously, but hesitated before saying anything else. He had been working closely with Gorza quite often in the days since Zesh had been defeated and fled with his supporters back to whatever clan they had come from. Taegan found he enjoyed her company, but still their interactions felt stilted and nervous. It was hard to build a friendly and casual rapport when the knowledge of Zorvut still asleep and recovering upstairs must have been in the back of both of their minds the whole time.

But, he thought, he at least had the benefit of feeling Zorvut's consciousness through the bond. Mostly, it was quiet, the way it would be anytime Taegan was awake while Zorvut slept, but occasionally he would have slight flashes of thoughts or emotions he couldn't quite place. But he knew those whispers were his husband dreaming, so there was some awareness there; all that could be done was wait for him to wake.

It was as simple as it was aggravating. But Gorza did not have that reassurance, and had hung onto every word from each healer and shaman who'd checked up on him, asking Taegan for updates each time she came by. Not that he could blame her; if anything, he was glad Zorvut had such a staunch ally in his sister, and by extension she was an ally to him as well.

"Anyway, that's all I have for now," Gorza said suddenly, breaking the silence that had settled over them. "Later today I'm checking with my contact in the mountain clans, so I may have news for you tonight, but they're so remote I don't expect much."

"Come by for dinner, then," Taegan offered as Gorza stood, and with a slight grin, she nodded.

"I will," she said. "Until then."

"Goodbye for now," Taegan replied, and she turned and left, leaving him sitting at the small table with a cup of tea and papers strewn around him.

He tried to busy himself with paperwork for a little longer, but it was proving difficult to focus on much of anything. He missed Zorvut, and his conversation with Gorza only made him feel it more acutely.

With a sigh, he stood and headed upstairs, leaving his shoes at the base of the stone steps to make his way barefoot up to their shared quarters. Their room was dark with the curtains drawn to block out the sun, but a few candles were lit to give the chamber a faint light. He was sure that the lighting made no difference, but there was a sense of normalcy to leaving the room dim while Zorvut slept, as if he were only napping and would be rousing soon.

Zorvut was right where Taegan had left him this morning and all the previous mornings, of course—laying on his back on the bed, propped up a bit with a few pillows and a light blanket pulled up to his shoulders. Each morning a healer had come by to examine him, moving his limbs to stretch his stationary muscles and switch out the blankets he laid upon, but they always returned with no new information. Just that he was healing, and his body would wake when it felt it could.

Taegan could not feel anything coming from the bond at the moment, but as he stepped up to Zorvut's side, it really did look like he was just resting. Like he might open his eyes and smile sleepily up at him if he were to only touch his arm.

He reached over to touch his shoulder, but there was no response. He did not truly expect one, but it was a slight disappointment all the same. With a sigh, Taegan pulled down the blanket enough to expose the length of Zorvut's arm, and with a bit of adjusting he could crawl into bed with his husband and nestle in the space between his arm and his chest.

"I miss you," he whispered, breathing in slowly and deeply to take in as much of the half-orc's comforting scent as he could. "Wake up soon, alright? We all need you. I can't rule in your stead forever. They're all waiting for you."

He tried to push all his love and longing toward the quiet spot in the back of his head where the bond slept. He had no idea how successful it might be, if Zorvut was aware of him at all, but he figured it couldn't hurt. As his eyes closed, he kept the bond cradled in his thoughts, letting every thought and feeling he had drift toward it as his breathing eventually slowed and he fell asleep.

Truly he had meant only to lie down for a bit and have the comfort of Zorvut's presence before getting back to work, but sleep overtook him before he realized, and then he was dreaming. He dreamt of a misty, grayish landscape, much like the hills outside Drol Kuggradh—rocky and almost bleak yet with a certain austere, untamed beauty about them. Standing in the center of the slopes was Zorvut, looking around—though he was not walking and there was no path in sight.

"Zorvut," he called out, but his voice was faint and distant, as if he were underwater. He frowned, feeling his throat; despite his muffled voice, though, Zorvut seemed to hear him and turned to look in his direction.

A moment ago, he had been watching Zorvut from afar, but he took one step and was now only perhaps ten feet away.

"I was wondering where you were," Zorvut said, and his head tilted with a curious expression. "I'm not sure how I got here."

"It's alright," Taegan said, and extended his hand. "Let's go home."

Zorvut looked at his hand, then turned to look back out at the mountains in the distance.

"I thought I heard..." he started, then trailed off. Taegan hesitated, then stepped forward to close the space between them, looping his outstretched hand around Zorvut's arm at his side as he peered up at him. "I don't know. I thought I heard something out there. Someone."

"Shall we go look?" Taegan asked, raising an eyebrow, but Zorvut shook his head quickly with a frown.

"No," he replied with an urgency that Taegan had not expected. "They were calling to me. Just me."

Distantly, Taegan thought the words should make him nervous. He did feel nervous, but it was far away—as if he were watching someone else become anxious rather than feeling it himself.

"Then let's go home," he said, squeezing Zorvut's arm a little more tightly. The half-orc's gaze lingered on the mist-covered mountains for a moment longer, scanning the horizon as if searching for something. But when he finally looked back down at Taegan, his gaze was brimming with adoration, and Taegan could not imagine why he would have ever doubted Zorvut would follow him.

"Yes," he agreed softly, pulling his arm from Taegan's grasp to wrap it around the elf's shoulders, pressing Taegan's body to him. "Let's go home."

They turned, and behind them was both the shape of Drol Kuggradh and, a short distance beyond it, the skyline of Aefraya with the castle on the high hill. Taegan laughed when he saw it in equal parts joy and surprise, and they stepped toward it at a leisurely pace.

As they walked, Taegan somehow knew, in the way dreams let him just know things without needing to see them, that their children were walking behind them hand-in-hand. He could hear their small voices, indistinct and formless, as they chattered and laughed, lagging behind them a little ways so that they could curiously inspect every flower and insect on their path. He did not need to turn to look back, but he knew they were there, and he was not worried.

As if sensing his thoughts, Zorvut glanced down at him, a fond smile on his face. His gaze was searching, as if he were waiting for Taegan to speak.

"We really can have it all, can't we?" Taegan said, returning the smile. Zorvut did not answer, but squeezed him a little tighter, and together they kept walking toward the cities in the distance. They walked in silence for a few minutes, only the crunch of their footsteps and the occasional lilting voices of their children behind them. But then Zorvut's arm around him tightened, squeezing him hard, and he looked up in surprise.

"What's wrong?" he asked, but when he looked, Zorvut was gone, and the landscape was silent. He was alone. He blinked in shock, turning behind him to look, and—

"Taegan," Zorvut's voice came softly, barely above a whisper, but still he could not see him. "Taegan?"

Taegan's eyes snapped open as he woke with a start. He was back in bed, his body still curled up next to Zorvut's torso, but now Zorvut was on his side facing Taegan, and when he looked his husband's golden-yellow eyes were staring back at him—sleepy, unfocused, but open.

Afraid he was still dreaming, Taegan slowly reached up to Zorvut's face, cupping it in both hands. Zorvut blinked, and his skin against Taegan's palms felt warm, alive, prickly with stubble.

"Taegan?" Zorvut said again, his voice the same hoarse whisper Taegan had heard in his dream.

His eyes overflowed with tears before he had even processed the words.

"You're awake," he choked out over a sob, wanting desperately to lean forward and kiss him, still afraid he might be dreaming or somehow hurt Zorvut if he moved too quickly. Already the dream was leaving his memory, and some part of him wanted to hold on to it, to remember, but the rest of him was overwhelmed with cautious joy. Zorvut was truly warm and alive in his arms. "You're really awake, aren't you?"

"I think so," Zorvut murmured, his eyes drifting around the room. His voice was gravelly with disuse, and he took in a few deep breaths before clearing his throat and speaking again. "What happened?"

"After the fight with Zesh, you—you passed out," Taegan replied, finally pulling one hand from Zorvut's face to wipe away his own tears. "You've been sleeping for a few days. The healers who looked at you, they all said you were hurt, but not too badly, and so your body must have just needed to rest."

Zorvut frowned, then groaned faintly.

"My back hurts," he said, wincing as he shifted against Taegan.

"Let's try and get you sitting up, alright?" he asked, and after a moment of hesitation, Zorvut nodded. Taegan got to his feet and gingerly helped Zorvut push himself into a sitting position, the blanket falling around his waist as he moved.

"I'm sore all over," Zorvut groaned, running a hand down his face before looking over at Taegan. "You said a few days?"

"Well, more like a week," Taegan replied with a chagrined expression, and Zorvut frowned.

"Has everything been alright?" he asked, glancing around the room again. "We're still in Drol Kuggradh?"

"We are," he agreed, nodding. He hesitated, unsure how much he wanted to explain with Zorvut still bleary and tired, but from the bond he could feel his concern and curiosity. So he took in a steady breath and continued, "Everything has been... fine, really. Gorza has been helping me a lot, but I've been working with Captain Kyrenic and some of the orc generals and merchants while you've been resting to make sure we can keep the peace. Truly, Zorvut, it's been going much more smoothly than I anticipated. You were right, you know—the orcs who live here, they just want to live their lives in peace. Once Zesh was gone, the few orcs who were still resistant went with him. We're not sure which clan they went back to, but I don't think they'll be causing any more problems, not anytime soon, at least. I've already sent messages back to Aefraya that we're now in control of Drol Kuggradh and... We've also started introducing new potential systems to the orcs here, floating the idea of a monarchy or something similar, like you were thinking of. There's going to be a public meeting where people can ask questions and such, and I'm sure it will be slow work, but I think it seems likely once everything settles, you're going to be king."

Zorvut was silent for a long moment, but Taegan could tell from the mix of emotions roiling in the bond that he understood everything he had told him. It was a lot to process, after all.

"That's a lot," Zorvut finally echoed softly, his eyes meeting Taegan's steadily. "I... I'm impressed, actually. Although I shouldn't be. Sometimes it's easy to forget you've trained your whole life to rule."

Taegan flushed at that, chuckling. "Well, that's true, but it's also because of Gorza's help. And all the other orcs I've worked with. They've made my job quite simple." His expression softened, and he sat next to Zorvut on the bed again. "Everyone has only the best things to say about you, my love. They want to work with me only because I'm working in your stead, and they want you to be the one in power. I'm absolutely sure you're going to be king."

Zorvut paused at that, seeming to ruminate over the words for a long moment.

"There's never been a king of the orcs before," he said softly. "And now there will be two." He frowned slightly and looked over at Taegan. "How will that work with Aefraya, your father?"

"We'll work with my father to figure something out," Taegan replied with a wry grin. "I'm surprised at how much you're concerned with the big picture so soon after waking up."

"So much has happened so quickly," Zorvut replied, shaking his head. "At least, that's how it feels. Gods, I'm sore." He moved as if trying to get out of bed, but stopped short quickly as a spark of pain shot through the bond. "Nngh—I forgot. Zesh... kicked me pretty hard."

Taegan winced, nodding. "I know, I saw. The healers that looked at you said there'd be no lasting damage, but, well..." He laughed nervously. "They recommended nothing, ah, intimate for a few weeks, unfortunately."

Zorvut let out a faint laugh, even though Taegan could tell he was still in pain. "Unfortunate," he agreed, squeezing his eyes closed. For a moment he remained completely motionless, then finally his muscles seemed to relax, and he leaned against his pillows again to lie back down. "Well, I'm awake, but I don't think I'll be going anywhere for a little while longer."

"That's alright," Taegan said quickly, resting a hand on Zorvut's forearm. "Take as long as you need to rest. Between me and Gorza, we'll be alright in the meantime."

A soft, contented fondness trickled through the bond as Zorvut smiled up at him. Despite everything, there was a peace in his eyes Taegan could not recall ever having seen before, and he couldn't help but return the smile. How could he not? His husband had come back to him. They were finally, finally together again—this time seemingly for good. Together, they would be kings, and they would achieve Zorvut's dream of uniting their kingdoms. How could he not be overcome with blind joy?

"Come here," Zorvut said softly, extending his arms, and Taegan leaned in to kiss him. There was nowhere else he'd rather be.

Epilogue

"Do I look alright?"

Zorvut's voice was nervous, an unsettled expression on his face when Taegan looked up at him in surprise at the question. Despite the anxious energy radiating from the bond, Taegan couldn't help but smile when their eyes met, which Zorvut hesitantly mirrored.

"You look incredibly handsome," he said, and it was the truth. His hair had grown out to nearly shoulder length, and he'd been keeping it in a similar half-shaved style like how it had been when they were first married, which Taegan had always found striking. He was dressed in a form-fitting tunic that had just been finished a few days before, a dark maroon with silver embroidery in sharp, angular designs that mirrored the strong angles of the crown that now sat upon his head. A thick and jagged piece wrought entirely of silver, it was artwork in its own right, and the minor peaks ascending up to the largest central point were reminiscent of the splendor of the mountain range always in the background of Drol Kuggradh, which was now their permanent home.

A slight flush crept up Zorvut's cheeks at the comment, but through the bond he felt pleased, if still rather embarrassed.

"It's not too much?" he asked, gesturing at the outfit. He tugged at the cord draped across his shoulders where his cape was attached, a thick, jet-black fabric that fell to his hips. "Maybe I should take off the cape."

"No, the cape makes you look quite dashing," Taegan said, stepping closer to fuss with his collar, although it didn't really need any adjusting. "Maybe it is a little more elven in fashion, though. Of course, I don't think anyone will get a good look at it while you're sitting."

Zorvut smirked at the remark, lifting his hands to hold Taegan's against his heart. He could feel the nervous pulse thrumming under his fingers. "I suppose I'll keep it, then."

His eyes flickered down past Taegan's hands to the baby held to his chest in a thick swath of dark cloth. "Still sleeping?"

"Yes, thank the gods," Taegan laughed, pulling back the folds of fabric so he could see. Nahara's face was pressed flush against the soft fabric of his robe, her eyes firmly closed in a deep sleep. Even from this angle, the tiny points of her ears poked through her soft black hair, but her ears seemed to be all she had inherited from Taegan as far as he could tell. Her dark hair, pale greenish-gray skin, and eyes that had steadily lightened to a honeyed yellow were all much more Zorvut in appearance.

The timing of her arrival had not exactly been ideal—she was just under a month old now. Their official coronation ceremony had been only three days ago and was the longest Taegan and Zorvut had been away from their daughter since she was born. Now, after the festival celebrations had died down, they would sit in the new throne room for the first time today to receive petitioners and welcome visiting nobles. But Taegan was loath to leave her, and so they had decided to keep her with them, at least for now.

Zorvut leaned down to gingerly press a feather-light kiss to the top of her head. Peering down at her for a moment, he shifted slightly, tilting his head up to then kiss Taegan, just missing his lips and instead kissing the corner of his mouth, eliciting a laugh from each of them.

"Hopefully she'll keep sleeping," Taegan said as Zorvut straightened, carefully pulling the fabric back over her face. "I'm glad my father decided to stay after the coronation ceremony. I'm sure he'd be happy to take her if she wakes."

"Not like anyone can tell us not to have her here," Zorvut mused, a grin lingering on his face.

Taegan laughed, shaking his head. "No, I suppose not, and she is the princess, after all. Still, it would be best to make a good impression on our first official day on the job."

"I expect you're right, as always," Zorvut nodded, taking a step back. "Really, it's not too much? I look alright?"

"Of course you do!" Taegan exclaimed. "Look at you. I love your hair at this length. The color suits you. And the crown..." He paused, a slight smile spreading across his face. "Well, it is intimidating, but in a good way."

"Hmm," Zorvut replied, smiling wryly in response. "I suppose I'll have to trust your opinion. Here, why don't you sit down? Are you tired?"

"Not at all," he said, shaking his head, but he sat down anyway, knowing his husband would fuss and worry over him until he did.

Though Zorvut would sit on the throne today, there was a second chair just beside it that he settled into. It was not quite as ornate, but was a bit more comfortable, so it was a sacrifice he was more than happy to make. They had already decided they would alternate who sat on the main throne, but Taegan thought it fitting for Zorvut to be the first to be seen upon it.

From the opposite end of the hall, three sharp knocks rapped on the wooden door. Zorvut frowned, glancing over his shoulder as the sound of it unlatching echoed through the empty chamber.

"I thought it wasn't supposed to be for another twenty minutes," he muttered, turning around, but when the door opened the figure following the elven guard was not an orc, or another elf, but a human.

"Tom!" Zorvut exclaimed, all but leaping in surprise as the man's familiar visage came into view, beaming at them. "What are you doing here?"

"I made it in time!" Tomlin Whitmore called out in response, the joy in his voice nearly palpable. His hair and beard were short-cropped and tidy as always, but the clothes he wore were much more formal than the casual wear they had only ever seen him in before, dark and silky and austere. "I just got here yesterday, missed all but the last few hours of the festival. Just my luck, of course. But more than that, I just wanted to see—to see you." He paused, still grinning, but he pressed his lips together tightly as if holding back tears. "And Taegan, of course. And is that...?"

Taegan stood quickly, though he had just sat down. "Yes, the little princess. Let me get her." He had hoped she would sleep through most of the morning, but Tom was looking at the soft bundle of cloth so eagerly that he couldn't deny him the chance to hold her now. Tom closed the distance between them, standing anxiously between Taegan and Zorvut as Taegan lifted down the layers of cloth and carefully retrieved their daughter from where she was pressed to his chest. Nahara stirred slightly as he lifted her out from the cloth wrap, but luckily stayed asleep as he placed her into Tom's waiting arms. He held her silently for a long moment, looking down at her sleeping features, before letting out a long, drawn-out sigh and hugging her gingerly with his lips pressed to her forehead.

"And to think it was hardly more than a year ago that I didn't even know you existed," he said softly, finally pulling his eyes away from his granddaughter to look up at Zorvut. "You've done... You've done extremely well for yourself, Zorvut."

The half-orc let out a bark of a laugh, shaking his head. "I owe much of it to you. And Taegan. I couldn't have accomplished any of this without help."

"I just want you to know I'm proud of you," Tom said quickly. "And I wanted to be here to see you, now that you're truly king. So you would know you'd always have my support. And, well..." He glanced back down at Nahara, grinning. "I certainly needed to meet the little one, too."

Zorvut nodded, and though his expression remained steady, from the bond Taegan could feel his heart overflow with pride. "Thank you. That means a lot to me. I'm glad you could come meet her so soon, too."

"You're welcome to stay as long as you'd like, of course," Taegan said smoothly. "In fact, my father is here as well. Perhaps the grandparents would like to meet?"

"Oh, gods, I don't know if I can handle meeting three kings in one day," Tom said with a laugh, shaking his head. "Here, I'll give her back to you. I know you're going to be busy soon. I just wanted to see you both."

"How long will you be in town?" Zorvut asked, though his eyes lingered on Nahara as Taegan took her back into his arms.

"Oh, I don't know," Tom said, shrugging. "I planned on a week, but I can stay longer. I'd love to spend as much time with you as you can spare, of course, but I know this is a busy time for you."

"It's no trouble at all," Zorvut said decisively. "I'll have guest quarters prepared for you. Whatever room you paid for last night, I'll cover it. You can stay as long as you'd like." He glanced back over at the doors, which were closed once more. The elven guard standing there, politely waiting for Tom, gave him a brief nod at the unspoken question. "But, unfortunately, we are just about to expect our first guests..."

"Of course, of course. Don't let me throw off your first day," Tom said, taking a quick step away. "And thank you for your hospitality. I'll be around, so call me up whenever."

"Join us for dinner tonight," Taegan said, and Tom nodded eagerly even as he was walking away.

"I'll plan on it," he said, and followed the elven guard back out the heavy double doors. Though the smile on his face was small and contained, Taegan could feel Zorvut was pleasantly surprised that Tom would be staying.

"Ready?" he asked as he turned back to Taegan. "Here, I'll help." Carefully they re-wrapped the baby against Taegan's chest, and though she wriggled a bit in protest, her eyes remained sleepily closed.

"I should be asking if you're ready," Taegan teased once he settled her back in place. "You're the one who's going to be doing most of the work today. I'm just here to look pretty." Zorvut laughed, shaking his head.

"I'll need you to do much more than that, my love," he said, leaning down to kiss him. Despite their joking rapport, the swell of emotions from the bond as their lips met was surprisingly tender.

"Where's this coming from?" Taegan asked, barely above a whisper, as Zorvut's lips hovered just above his own. He could feel his husband smile against him.

"I'm happy," Zorvut replied softly. "I have everything I've ever wanted and more. I hope I feel this way every time I kiss you, forever."

"An ambitious goal, King Zorvut," Taegan replied, smiling. "I'll do what I can to help you in achieving it."

"That's all I ask, King Taegan," Zorvut said, and with that, he took a step back. "Well, we don't want to be running late on our first day."

"Certainly not! In fact, early is on time, as far as I'm concerned. I'm ready when you are," Taegan agreed, sitting back down in his chair as Zorvut stepped up to the throne. He watched as the half-orc scanned it with his eyes for a long moment, the weight of everything seeming to settle on his shoulders all at once, then with a deep breath, he sat down as well.

In the morning light streaming through the many windows in the chamber, Zorvut looked positively resplendent sitting on the throne, the sun giving his eyes a golden glow and illuminating the silvery crown with bright, gleaming rays. At his side, with the warm bundle of their baby pressed to his skin... Just as Zorvut had said, it really was everything he had ever wanted, and more. Here, everything felt right, like a long journey finally coming to an end.

Zorvut met his eyes with a small smile, and Taegan nodded. With a wave of his hand, Zorvut turned his attention back to the guard awaiting his command at the door. "Send them in."

THE END

About the Author

Lionel Hart (he/him) is an indie author of MM fantasy romance and paranormal romance. Currently, he resides in north San Diego with his husband and their dog. For personal updates and new releases, follow the links below.

Twitter: @lionelhart_

Facebook: Lionel Hart, Author

TikTok: @author.lionelhart

Email Newsletter

Also By Lionel Hart

Chronicles of the Veil

1. The Changeling Prophecy

2. The Drawn Arrow

The Orc Prince Trilogy

1. Claimed by the Orc Prince

2. Blood of the Orc Prince

3. Ascension of the Orc King

Heart of Dragons Duology

1. Beneath His Wings

Lightning Source UK Ltd.
Milton Keynes UK
UKHW011810140622
404428UK00002B/450